CW01066464

HEART
OF THE
ISLAND

DAVID KONRAD

To Lisa, who made this book possible, and to Viktor and Gabriel, who almost made it impossible, but for whom I wrote it.

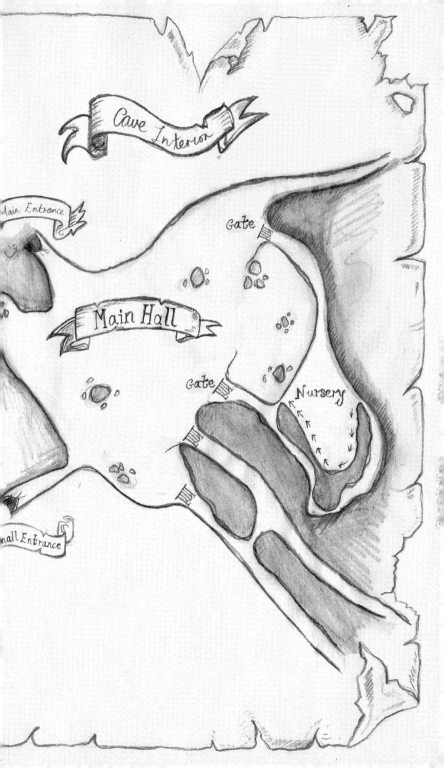

PROLOGUE

SOME YEARS AGO

Jacob Davenport was staring into the eyes of a man who was about to make his family much less rich. Gambling was his biggest vice, and even though his wife and his daughter Luisa begged him to stop, he had gotten himself into a tight situation, yet again.

'You're just bluffing,' he muttered.

The face of the man sitting across the table from him opened in a wide grin, showing a missing front tooth.

'Maybe. Or maybe not. Your call, my friend!' the man snickered.

The room they were sitting in wasn't too small, but it was very crowded. The amount of money at stake in the poker game had brought many spectators. They all shuffled on the wooden floor as close as they could get to see the action. The air was thick with smoke. All the lights in the room were dimmed, except the one hanging directly above the poker table. Five players were sitting around it, three of them out of this pot already.

Jacob was holding great cards in his hand. Great cards. But not the best possible cards. No. There was a chance, although small, that he might lose this one. He didn't need the money. His family was rich—they'd been rich for centuries. But he was a gambler, and sometimes he just couldn't help himself.

'I think I should call your bluff,' he said in a very calm and confident voice, but feeling very differently inside.

'I don't think you have enough money on the table to call me,' the man said, narrowing his eyes. 'I think you should reconsider it,' he taunted Jacob.

'Maybe I don't have the money right now, but you know I'm good for it.'

'Now how would I know that? All I see is a guy with a small stack of cash in front of him.'

'Well, maybe we could work something out. I do have other valuables at my house, and more cash in the bank.'

The man sat there for a while, studying Jacob's face. Finally, he said, 'You know what I want. It's what I've always wanted. I want the Heart.'

Jacob knew that he did. Everybody did—

the Heart of the Island was one of the biggest diamonds that had ever been found in the rich mines around the town of Lakeview, and the Davenport family had owned it ever since.

'You know that's not going to happen,' Jacob said, unsure of himself. 'I know you're bluffing, but I can't—no, *I won't* call your bluff with that. Not the Heart.'

'Suit yourself,' the man said, and reached for the pile of cash in the middle of the table.

'Wait!' Jacob cried. He could not believe what he was doing. Was he really about to bet his family's most valuable possession?

'Just wait, will you? Let me think for a second . . . '

***

On the way back to the Davenport Island Mansion, Jacob's mind raced despite the overwhelming roar of his small outboard motor.

Oh my god, what have I done? he kept thinking. He felt like the dark waters of the lake were closing in on him. As if he was driving the boat deeper and deeper beneath the surface. He had done a terrible thing, and now he had only a week to come up with a ridiculous amount of money, or he'd have to give up the Heart of the Island. That was the deal he made, and there was no way of escaping it—there had been far too many witnesses, including the town's mayor. No. He had to pay his debt. But he couldn't give up the diamond—it was too precious, and his family would never forgive him, especially his daughter.

I have to hide that diamond, he thought, *I can't be the one to lose it!*

He knew that he could get the money by selling some of the other jewelry from the big safe in the house, but he was still worried about the Heart. The man to whom he'd lost the poker game appeared to be very keen on getting his hands on it. Jacob didn't trust that man. He seemed like he wanted the Heart more than anything. And Jacob knew about the man and his criminal past, and the dark stories people told about him.

So, maybe it was the reassuring image of the beautiful Davenport Island Mansion looming in the darkness, or just the fresh, cool night air that helped him come up with an idea. Jacob didn't know, but he thought that it might actually work. He allowed himself a small grin, as he pondered more on the idea.

The boat quickly reached the small dock, and

Jacob jumped off confidently. Strength returned to his legs, his back straightened up, and he marched toward the house feeling like a man with a plan.

***

The next day Jacob made sure everybody in Lakeview knew he was going to the city to take care of some urgent business. The news about Jacob losing the game, and possibly the diamond, had spread like wild fire since early in the morning. Even the mayor came down to the dock to see and talk to Jacob, while Jacob's driver was packing the car and getting it ready for the long drive to the city.

'Well, Mr. Davenport, I assume you're going to the bank in the city to get the cash you owe to the gentleman from last night's game?' the mayor asked.

'You assume correctly, Mr. Mayor,' Jacob said as clearly as he could, and as loudly as he dared. 'But that's not all—I'm going to put the Heart of the Island diamond in the safe in my bank in the city. I believe it will be safer there than it is on our small island, if you know what I mean.'

Jacob was satisfied with the reaction he got

from the mayor, and other people listening in to the conversation. They seemed to believe him. The gossip will spread as quickly as the news about the last night's game—he was sure of that. He signaled to the driver that he was ready, and he let himself onto the back seat. The drive would be a few hours long, and he still had things to work out in his head.

Later that evening, when he returned from the bank with the cash to pay his debt, there were far fewer people interested in him as his driver dropped him off at the dock. He jumped in his boat, and started the motor. He liked the idea of 'hiding in plain sight,' and he felt pretty good about the cover story with the bank. Still, he wasn't entirely sure where to hide the diamond. It *has to be hidden on the island. It just has to— the island is its home,* Jacob thought to himself, staring forward at the fast-approaching island. *But where on the island to hide it, exactly?*

THIS YEAR

1

Dad was driving the car like he wanted to get to the lake as late as possible. It wasn't such a long ride to begin with, but he really made it seem like it took forever. Even my mom looked like she was bored and annoyed. And she liked road trips. She was sprawled on the passenger's seat next to him, her bare feet perched on the dashboard, an empty soda can in her hand. The morning was getting hotter, but the car's windows were all closed tight, and the AC was running full blast. The car was packed full, even though we were just going on a weekend trip to a lake not too far from my hometown. Apart from all our food and clothes, my dad had bought brand new fishing equipment, which needed to be tested, and there was a pretty big canoe strapped to the roof of our car.

I squirmed on the back seat behind Dad, and looked out the windshield, through the straps holding the canoe tight in place on both sides of the hood. We were getting closer. I could see the mountains clearly now, almost close enough to pick out individual trees.

'Look at this,' Matt bumped my arm with his elbow, and pointed at some impossibly boring rock in his geology book. That's Matt Sharkey, by the way, my best friend. We're neighbors, and we grew up together, and we play basketball together, and—well, you get the picture. The thing is though, we couldn't be more different in so many ways. We even look different. He is *almost* as tall as me, almost, but he is a bit stronger—I'll give him that. And I like my hair short, really short. Like buzzcut short. Matt wears this black, curly thing that looks like a bird's nest on top of his head—not short, not long.

'The book says that this Zircon is the oldest rock on Earth—' he continued, but then stopped when he realized I was glaring at him like he'd gone crazy. He glanced at me with his dark, almost black eyes, and decided I wasn't all that interested in old rocks. It was my mom's idea to get him this book for his twelfth birthday last week, and now I'm suffering for it.

'Book hater,' he muttered, his eyes staring back at his precious book. I really liked Matt, but he was such a nerd sometimes. He always loved to read all the kids' encyclopedias, all the books about animals, about the weather, about machines and computers, and now—about rocks and dirt.

I turned my gaze out the window again, and shifted in my seat. UnfortunateIy, I took the seat behind my dad, which meant even less legroom. And after being in the car for the past couple of hours I was feeling it. I knew Matt and I were going to be sleeping on bunk beds at the lake cabin, and I really hoped that the beds would be a decent size. I really hated tight spaces, and they always made me feel trapped and uncomfortable—almost claustrophobic. Also, they say I'm a very energetic kid—always running around doing something, tons of energy—so you can see why I hated tight spaces. And, unlike Matt, who's like this quiet philosopher or something, I like to talk a lot, and my mind is always racing —

'There's the lake, we're almost there! Ethan, can you please keep your knees out of my back?' Dad called out from the driver's seat.

That's my name, by the way, Ethan Gilmour, and I am still eleven, with my twelfth birthday a few weeks from now. I hope my mom won't have a similar idea for a present for me—I would much prefer a new bike, or even a pair of nice brand-new Jordan basketball shoes! Like I said, I'm not much of a bookworm, but I really love being outdoors, getting myself into trouble, going on adventures if I can. Although there are a few things that still freak me out, courage is not in short supply for me. And usually, when I do get myself into trouble, Matt is there with his giant brain to help me get out of it. Did I mention he's very book-smart?

Anyway, soon I felt the car slowing down, and finally, we turned down the slip road toward Lakeview.

As we got closer to the town, we took yet another small road toward the cabin my parents had rented from a local owner. After a short, slow ride, through the thin woods, I could already see the cabin and behind it the lake glistening in the morning sun.

There was a short driveway through the woods to the cabin. My dad turned into it, slowly, keeping his eyes planted on the edge of the ragged asphalt. Then, from the outside of the car, we heard a loud snapping crack, and the whole car shuddered as Dad stepped on the brakes.

'Stop! Watch out!' Mom cried, as she looked up at the canoe through the windshield. The brand-new canoe strapped to the roof of our car now lay at an angle. Well, actually it was still aiming forward, in direction of the road, but it was stuck to a large branch hanging down from a tree. We all climbed out of the car, eyes looking up, bodies bent down, worried that it could fall on our heads.

Dad checked the car for damage, while Matt and I took the canoe off the roof and hauled it down the short dirt driveway to the cabin. When Dad was satisfied with how the car looked, he drove it down to the cabin, even more slowly than before. Matt and I joined him at the car and started unloading the stuff.

The cabin was a simple two-story wooden structure, with a long and narrow porch, and a fantastic view of the lake. Off to the left, I could see a sliver of the main beach through the scattered pine trees.

'Dibs on the top bunk,' I said, running into the small bedroom on the bottom floor. Matt just shrugged. He couldn't care less. We put our stuff down in the room, and went to explore the rest of the building. The whole cabin smelled like the forest itself. Like it was still a living part of it, not just made from it. I almost expected to see leaves growing out of the wooden beams. I walked up the stairs, and just quickly peeked into the master bedroom where Mom was already neatly filling the wardrobe with her clothes, and Dad lay down on the bed, eyes closed, winding down from the road. Apart from the main bathroom, there was only one other room upstairs, and Matt was already standing at its door. He opened it, with me following right behind and we walked into something that must have been somebody's study room, or a library.

The room had floor-to-ceiling bookshelves covering two of the walls with hundreds of books stacked on them. There was a small cabinet in the corner to the left, and a large wooden desk placed in the center, facing the door. Behind the desk there was a big glass sliding door, taking up most of the wall. I could hear the sound of kids having fun down at the beach, and I started to wonder why we weren't there yet.

'Who owns this place, anyway?' Matt asked, while looking at some framed photos hanging on the back wall. 'And who's she?'

I glanced back and saw a photo of an older woman, and a much younger version of her, smiling together for the camera in front of some old castle, probably in Europe somewhere.

'Mom said the place belongs to some Davenport woman or something like that. It's supposed to be really old, like, a hundred years old or something. My guess is that's her in the picture, maybe with her granddaughter?' I offered. 'But who cares? Let's go check out the beach!'

'Yeah. Hold on a sec. Come check this out', Matt stared at a map on the wall. 'There's an island on this lake, but come check out the name. Cool.'

I put a book I was leafing through back down on the desk and joined Matt at the wall. The map showed not much more than the lake itself, with just parts of the surrounding mountains, and Lakeview to the west. In the middle of the lake there was a small island with some buildings on it. I leaned closer, and read aloud the name written across the top of the island: 'The Dead-end Island.'

I rolled my eyes at Matt, and sniffed at the map. 'Wow. Somebody watched too many movies—'

'Can I help you boys with anything?' A quiet, raspy voice demanded from the door frame. Then the door swung all the way open, and the woman from the photos walked in, her green eyes darting suspiciously between Matt and me.

2

'I, I mean we—I mean— we're just looking around!' I blurted. Matt said nothing.

'You boys shouldn't snoop around. There are valuable books and art in here, so better if you just keep out of this room, do you understand?' she said.

She didn't look scary at all—she was small and white-haired and wrinkled, but her voice sent chills down my spine. She sounded like a mafia hitman from bad TV shows or movies.

'I didn't know we're not supposed to come here,' I continued, as I raised my hands in defense. 'We were just checking out the rest of the house.'

She nodded, and softened a little.

'All right, all right, don't worry about it. Just make sure you don't make a mess up here, ok? And I'm sorry I startled you boys. I know my voice sounds scary, but I can't help it—it's what happens when you get old and sick.' She winked, and her green eyes smiled at us. 'I'm Ms. Davenport, but you can call me Luisa. And how may I call you, gentlemen?'

We introduced ourselves, already warming to the old lady.

'What were you kids interested in?' she said as she started to pull some books off the shelves and placed them into a neat pile on top of the desk.

'We were looking at this map here on the wall,' said Matt, finally joining the conversation. 'Why is that island called Dead-end Island?'

She turned and looked at the map for a long moment before answering. Her eyes had lost the smile and I could sense she wasn't just being sad. Her jaw clenched as she dealt with memories from a long time ago.

'It wasn't always called that, you know. It once belonged to my family, and it was called Davenport Island. But my father —' she paused a beat, then sighed. 'Let's just say that he made some really bad decisions in his life, and the island doesn't belong to the family anymore. It's a fancy hotel now, being renovated.'

Then, a piercing shriek burst through the open glass door and filled the small, crowded room. It startled us all, and we turned our heads toward the windows. It sounded like it came from the beach.

Matt was first to react. He swung the sliding door open and we stumbled onto the small balcony. Ms. Davenport came out right behind us. I squinted at the brilliant, glistening lake, protecting my eyes with my hand. The morning sun bouncing off of it made it impossible to look directly at the water. Off to the right, in the middle of the lake, the small island looked like a hole in a bright, shiny mirror. To the left of the cabin, toward Lakeview, I could see the main beach. There were some kids sitting on the beach and some were goofing around in the water.

'I thought I recognized that voice.' Ms. Davenport said, shaking her head in amused disapproval. 'That's Karen, my granddaughter. And those two scallywags are probably her cousins. I can't really see that well all the way from here, but I think that's Jason right next to her. They must've scared her somehow—they're always on the lookout for mischief.'

I took a better look and saw Karen, who was probably the girl from the photos, giggling in the shallow water. She was splashing the two boys who stood next to her, retaliating for the scare. There were a few other kids at the beach, laughing at the scene, obviously all part of the same group of friends.

'I guess we should be down there too,' I said. 'We should go and meet those kids. Matt? What do you think? A test run with the canoe, and see if we can say hi to them?'

'Ok,' Matt shrugged, in his own, unique, uninterested way. 'In a minute—I want to hear more about the island, please. Why was it named Dead-end Island?'

Ms. Davenport turned to him, looking surprised at the question. As if she'd forgotten that she was telling the story about her father, Jacob Davenport, and the island.

'Well —' she drifted back to her memories again, 'there is a cave system on that island. And many people got lost in those tunnels, coming to dead ends. One man was never found, or heard of, ever again. He must've disappeared in those caves. They were all searching for something down there, something that belonged to my family . . . '

The expression of sorrow and resentment crept back into Ms. Davenport's face, and I knew it was time to leave her alone and say goodbye. As we were leaving the room, she gave us an eerie warning.

'Boys, do not go into those caves without a guide, no matter what you hear about it. It's very dangerous and you might get lost!'

I glanced at Matt, and because of the look he gave me, I knew right away we were going to visit those caves, one way or the other.

3

'Mom! Dad! We're going down to the beach!' I yelled, not really caring if anybody heard me. 'We're taking the canoe!'

Matt and I had changed quickly in our room and were now ready to go to the water. The late morning sun was already turning the day into a furnace, and it was getting hotter and hotter, even in the shade of the tall trees scattered around the cabin.

'Hold up, mister,' Mom said as she stopped us, coming out of the kitchen. 'You two are not going anywhere near that canoe without the vests. And right now, I don't see either one of you wearing one!'

'They're in the canoe, Mom. Don't worry, we'll be safe—it's just a little lake, it's not like there are big waves or anything!'

And it was true. We'd put the bright orange life vests in the canoe while unloading the car, and now we were ready to go. I grabbed my backpack, Matt tossed a pair of paddles in the canoe, and we started flip-flopping down a narrow pathway toward the beach. The tall pines provided us with shade while we 'partner-carried' the canoe, as Matt pointed out. For a guy that didn't say much, he really said a lot of weird stuff like that.

We walked all the way down the narrow trail and a few minutes later emerged from the thin woods. A narrow patch of grass quickly turned into a gravel beach. We shuffled toward the water, the canoe already feeling heavy in our hands. A few feet from the waterline, the gravel gave way to fine sand, and the water looked clean and clear and very inviting.

We put the canoe down just out of the water, and stretched our sore shoulders. I set my backpack on the gravel behind us and took a deep breath. The earthy smell of the lake water brought a smile to my face, and I exhaled slowly. I looked around and noticed that the beach had gotten quieter. The only thing I could hear was the faint roar of a jackhammer, probably coming from the renovation works at the island. The hot sun, now high in the sky, had chased the kids off the beach, and they were now sprawled in the shade under the trees playing card games. There were two canoes pulled out on the other side of the beach, probably belonging to those kids.

'I'm getting in!' I announced, as I shook the flip-flops off my feet. I took off my sweat-drenched T-shirt, and tossed it over the backpack. My face turned into a huge grin, and so did Matt's, as we ran into the water together, screaming all the way until we hurled ourselves in. I swam under the water for a few seconds, my eyes piercing through the clear bluish-green water. The water felt perfect on my overheated body as I stood up in the shallow lake, just hanging out there, taking in the majestic scenery. The whole place looked like a postcard—tall mountains crumbling down into a beautiful oval lake, the rocky mountain tops transforming sharply into dense pine tree forests, thinning out as they reached the grassy meadows at the waterline.

'So? When are we gonna check that out?' Matt nodded his head in the direction of the island. Of course. I knew that the island and its caves was the only thing on his mind since Ms. Davenport had told us her crazy treasure story.

'Nuh-uh. I'm not going over there. There's nothing to see there—you know I'm not interested in caves?' I said, barely managing to keep my face straight.

'Yeah, ok. Like I believe you. So, when are we going?' Matt didn't even turn to look at me—he always knew when I was messing with him.

'I don't know. Not now, I guess. We don't have any shoes with us, just flip-flops. Or a flashlight. Or anything else we might need. And we're supposed to be back for lunch soon. My mom will go ballistic if we don't show up on time.'

'Ok,' he nodded. 'But let's take the canoe out on the water now, I want to take a closer look at the island.'

I had nothing against the idea—I wanted to check out the island and test the canoe myself. So after a few crazy jumps and somersaults in the shallows, some more spraying and howling, we turned to half swim, half walk back to the beach. It was then that we noticed that two of the kids from the group we saw at the beach earlier were standing next to our canoe, staring at us. Their big arms were crossed as they waited for us to get out of the water.

4

I recognized the two cousins Ms. Davenport talked about on the balcony at the cabin, and immediately noticed their green eyes and blond hair—Davenport family trait, I guessed.

We walked out of the lake and headed straight toward the canoe and our stuff lying next to it. I felt uneasy, and wondered what it was they wanted. But I could already smell trouble. Just like Matt, I never *liked* fighting, but neither one of us would run away from it, so we got ourselves ready to stand our ground, if necessary.

The two boys were maybe a year or two older than us, just as tall, but bigger, wider in the shoulders. The guy on the left, Jason Davenport, looked very strong, and his whole body looked like a tree trunk. His arms were also huge, his muscles bulging under his tanned skin. His head was covered with blonde bowl-cut hair, bleached almost white by the sun. The guy on the right, Will Davenport, was almost a carbon copy of Jason. He had slightly darker hair, but I couldn't tell if it was only because he'd stayed out of the sun a little bit more. His ears were bigger and stuck away from his head, and his eyes were placed a bit closer together, all of which made him look dumb and mean. Not a good combination, I thought, as Jason called out to us.

'You kids think you can swim in our lake for free?' he said.

'Or maybe you think you can take this tub out without paying for the 'lake canoeing license'?' Will added, a smirk on his face, as he glanced at my canoe.

Matt was quiet as usual, but not stepping back, either. I swallowed hard and said, 'This isn't your lake,' my voice sounding feeble and shaky—or at least it did to me. 'So leave us alone. We're not paying anything to anyone.'

I could feel my voice coming back a little. *Good*, I thought to myself, I would need my voice to call for help when they sit on me and pound my head into the sand.

'Is your mommy making you wear those little kids' vests?' Will continued, noticing our life vests in the canoe.

'I don't think you two understand,' Jason stepped closer. 'I'm not *asking* you to pay us, I'm *telling* you!'

Now both of them took another step nearer, their feet and hands set wide apart, menacingly.

'Jason! Will!' we heard a girl's voice cry out, and saw Ms. Davenport's granddaughter, Karen, rushing toward us over dry, scorched grass at the top of the beach from amongst the group of kids sitting in the shade. They were all on their feet now, gazing in our direction, watching the show. Luckily for us, Karen seemed to have noticed that there was something going on, and was hopefully coming to bail us out.

'What's going on here?' she demanded.

'None of your business. Go back up there,' Will said, shooing her away with his hand.

'Like that's gonna happen,' Karen said, firmly. 'What is up with you two? Why do you always have to pick on city kids at the beach? Don't you have anything better to do?'

What did she mean by 'city kids'? Is it that obvious? I thought. *Do we look that pale?* I didn't know, but I did straighten my back, and tried to keep my chest forward. Not because of the girl, of course, that'd be silly. Just to appear bigger and tougher for the two bullies.

'Do you want me to call your parents and tell them what you're doing here? I'm sure you'd enjoy spending the rest of your summer back in the city,' Karen continued, paying little attention to the quiet, menacing stares both Jason and Will had aimed at her.

But after a few edgy, intense moments, they slowly turned back to us, and Jason snarled, *'This is not over.'* As they finally started walking away, Will turned to Karen, his eyes narrowing. He pointed his finger at her and half-whispered, *'You're a traitor! We'll get you for this!'*

5

'Hi. I'm Karen. And those two are my cousins, unfortunately,' she said as she offered her hand for a handshake. We introduced ourselves, still upset by what had just happened. Well, at least I was upset, I didn't know anything about what was going on in that robot head of my friend's. He just looked calm, as he always did.

'Thanks. I mean, you know—for helping us back there,' I managed to mumble. 'Can you tell us what that was about?'

'Yeah. Don't worry about it. Those two are always picking on some younger kids—they do it every summer. They think it's fun, but I've had enough of that,' Karen shook her head in disapproval, as if she had to apologize for them.

'I thought they were picking on us because we're from the city, and they're some kind of locals, showing off,' I said.

'No—we're all city kids here. Their parents

work in the city, just like mine, while we spend our summers at our grandmother's house,' Karen explained. 'You guys are here just for the weekend, right? Your mom rented that cabin from my grandmother.'

'Yeah,' I nodded. 'And we met your grandmother earlier. Nice lady. Told us some old stories . . . '

'Really? What kind of stories?' she prompted, wanting to know more.

'Something about her father and the caves on the island. And people looking for something in them,' I said.

'Really?' Karen raised her eyebrows, and paused for a beat, like she was figuring out how to proceed. 'She told you that silly old story? You shouldn't believe everything you hear, you know that?'

'Yeah, right, whatever. She didn't really say much,' I mumbled under my breath and shrugged my shoulders.

'Anyway, what are you guys up to? Wanna hang out with us? Meet the others?' she continued nodding her head toward the group of kids in the shade.

I wouldn't usually say no to hanging out with a pretty girl like Karen. And she was pretty—

very pretty. She had beautiful teeth, white and brilliant, although her lips seemed to be a bit too thin for her face. Her hair was tied in a wet ponytail, but I could see it was long and straight. And unsurprisingly, blond. She had green eyes too, like other members of that weird family, but hers were special. They were the kind of eyes that make you wanna ask if they're real or maybe contacts or something.

But I kind of wanted to get away from that beach and the other kids. I still felt all shook up by the threats made by Jason and Will. And Matt seemed to think the same. I glanced at him, and he gave me a shrug. It was a kind of shrug that only I could see and understand, meaning he would rather go out on the water.

'Thanks, but actually we wanted to go check out the lake and the island in my canoe. It's brand new, and we still haven't tried it out,' I finally said. 'You can join us if you want?' *Wow. Did I really say that? That sounded totally lame, didn't it?*

Anyway, she simply declined the invitation and said something about having to help her grandmother. She said she'd see us later, swung back and left toward the group of kids loitering among the trees.

Matt and I pulled on our vests, put the canoe in the water and climbed in. We pushed our paddles against the bottom of the lake to reach water deep enough to start paddling for real. Then we headed straight toward the island, which I figured would take us about ten or fifteen minutes to reach. I was sitting in the front, and Matt was in the back, being the heavier of the two of us. He'd read somewhere that it was better for balance and stability of the canoe if the heavier person sits in the back. I didn't mind—with him as quiet as he always was, it felt like I was all alone in a boat on a beautiful lake. We didn't even talk much about what had happened on the beach, and I was guessing we'd be okay for just that weekend. I was hoping Karen's intervention would keep us safe.

I was lulled into the rhythm of paddling, squinting into the sun and enjoying the views of the beautiful mountains around the lake, when suddenly the canoe jerked one way, and then the other. The mountains went flipping over, the paddle flew right out of my hands, and the surface of the lake came charging at my face. I hit the water hard, and the canoe toppled over me, as I found myself upside down in the water.

6

It took a long moment to figure out where the surface was. Then I saw the glare of the sun piercing through the clear water. I started frantically kicking my legs and stroking with my arms, swimming toward the glare. The vest didn't help at all—it got pulled over my head, so when I surfaced, I had to pull it further down my body first to get to the air. I guess I didn't tie it up well enough. When I managed to get some air into my gasping lungs, I looked around to try to understand what had happened. We were floating in our vests in the middle of the lake. My canoe was toppled over, and our plastic paddles were floating away from it, propelled by the ripples in the water.

Matt was laughing hysterically, barely keeping himself afloat and his mouth dry.

'Hey! What's wrong with you?! That's not funny!' I cried, but already getting over it. It was kind of funny, and we started laughing together, spraying each other, wrestling and trying to dunk each other's head under the water. 'Wait,' I suddenly realized, 'where's my backpack?!' I shrieked in total panic. Forget about the water and sunscreen in it – our PHONES were in it!

Matt laughed even harder. At that point I wanted to grab one of the paddles and smack him on his head with it. But I wasn't sure that would even hurt him, because of his black curly mop that seemed to have stayed dry and firm, somehow, like a bike helmet.

'I left it on the beach,' he managed to utter between the laughs. 'What, you think I'm that stupid?'

'YES!' I exclaimed. But I didn't really think that. I was mad at him for leaving the phones and our stuff on the beach, but also relaxing a bit, knowing they weren't at the bottom of the lake. He just kept laughing. Then I realized we had another problem. Like, how do you get back in a canoe that's been toppled over in the middle of a lake?

Matt was back to his serious self again, and he swam to the other end of the canoe. 'We need to flip it over first,' he said.

No kidding, I thought. 'Ok, let's flip it to my

left, one, two, three—.' Flipping the canoe over was easy, but now we had to get back in. 'Any bright ideas now—genius?' I asked Matt, since he was the one who put us into this mess in the first place.

'Yeah. It's easy. First just go to the other side,' he said, as he pulled himself along the canoe to the widest part in the middle. 'Now we just pull ourselves in, but best if we go at the same time. That will keep it stable, I hope.'

So we did. And it was easy—piece of cake. No idea why I doubted Matt at all. Still, just to get one over on him after flipping us over, I smacked my paddle on the water right next to him, making sure his face received most of the splashing water.

We continued paddling toward the island, as the sun shone down on us almost vertically now. I could hear the loud chirp of the crickets coming from the island. It seemed louder than on the shores of the lake, but maybe it was just because the jackhammer roar had stopped, and it was suddenly much quieter out here. When we almost reached the small beach and a dock next to it, we turned left to paddle clockwise around the island. There was a medium-sized inflatable boat pulled out on the beach, and a larger one, like a barge or something, tied to the dock. I guessed the inflatable dingy was used by the security guy we could now see talking to some workers, and the barge was there for the workers and their tools and machines. The security guy didn't pay any attention to us. He glanced at us, and just turned his head back to talk to a guy wearing a bright yellow hard hat. I supposed he would have been more interested in us had there been famous guests at the fancy hotel at the time.

Off to the right of the dock, a stone walkway was leading away from the lake and toward the house. The big house, a mansion, stood surrounded by beautiful landscaped gardens, and there were even small fountains scattered at short intervals, but there was no stream of water—probably shut down for renovation.

As we paddled close along the waterside off to the left and past the small beach, we saw a dense growth of bushes closer to the shore and some small trees scattered around the island interior. Just a few paces from the waterline, mostly hidden from prying eyes by a dense hedge, there was a narrow gravel pathway, and it looked like it encircled the entire island. A nice place to go for a walk in the evening—if you're rich and famous.

It was difficult to see much from the canoe, but through the few small openings in the hedge I could see the back of the mansion. Not far from it, I could see a batch of small buildings, probably used by the staff, and a clearing between them and the big house. The concrete-paved clearing had a big 'H' painted on it, and was obviously used as a helipad, but now it had some old wooden office furniture dumped all over it, that looked like it had just been cleared out.

We quickly paddled halfway around the island, and there we saw a clearing in the shrubbery on a small slope. At that point we were in the shadow of the island, and we couldn't see our cabin anymore. On top of the little slope there was a steel-barred gate of some sort, mounted on a rock frame of a tunnel, with a small tasteful flower garden in front of it, and a few wooden benches scattered around.

'Is that the cave entrance?' I said, more to myself than as a question.

'Looks like it. There, can you see the board?' Matt had his paddle in his lap, and was pointing his finger up to the gate.

'Yeah. But I can't read what it says. What's up with those steel bars? What are those for?' I asked.

'Beats me. But you know what? We should go. I'm starving!' As Matt said that, I suddenly realized that I was starving too, and I didn't have to be told twice. We paddled the rest of the way around the small island, noticing nothing more than what we'd already seen, and then we started paddling back across the lake, straight toward our cabin and the beach. When we got there, all the kids were gone, and so were Karen and her bully cousins, but my dad was standing on the beach, right there at the waterline. His arms were crossed. He was obviously waiting for us, and he looked angry.

7

'Where have you two been? I've been looking all over for you! Your mother is worried sick. You know better than this!' That last part was aimed straight at me. I knew Matt would be ok—in the eyes of my parents he could do nothing wrong— it was always me.

'But Dad —'

'But nothing! I don't want to hear it! Where are your phones? I called you first, but then she made me go look for you. We couldn't see you at the beach, we had no idea where you were!'

I glanced at the backpack Matt left out on the beach. Then I looked at Matt, to see if he'd step up. He did, thankfully, or I would have had to end our friendship right there.

'I'm sorry, I forgot to put the backpack in the canoe. The phones are in there,' Matt said in an apologetic voice, pointing at the backpack a few feet behind my dad.

Dad turned to look, but he was already calming down and losing interest in the whole thing. I guess Mom made him get up from reading his book or something to go look for us, and now he just wanted to get back in the shade and cool of the cabin.

We put the paddles in the canoe and left it all right there on the beach. My dad walked in front of us, fast, and we quietly followed. At the cabin, my mom said pretty much the same things as my dad did at the beach, so I just stood still and said '*I'm sorry*' a couple more times. Matt just kept quiet.

'They're too young to go paddling around like this. It's dangerous!' she said to Dad.

'Come on . . . It's not that dangerous. Besides, they will promise to keep those vests on, and to have the phones with them, in their waterproof bags—always! Right boys?' Dad managed to calm her down, and she was finally ok with that promise. We sat down to have lunch, and Dad started talking about the fishing book he was reading.

'Did you guys know they have Northern Pike in this lake, which grow up to three feet long?!' he told us, excited like a little kid. 'The best time to catch 'em is early in the morning, before the sun is up. I gotta get outta here around four in the morning!'

'Well, that means we'll be going to bed early tonight. I expect you guys to be quiet when we go to sleep,' Mom added, and I just nodded, still feeling guilty.

After lunch, and maybe because of the sun, I felt like taking a little nap, and Matt said he'd join me. The cabin had two hammocks on its porch, one in each corner. I liked that distance between them, because it meant I might not hear Matt's deafening snoring. We climbed in, and the heat of the early afternoon, the smell of the pine trees and the relentless concert of crickets soon made my eyelids feel as heavy as lead.

Suddenly, the day turned into night, and all the light was gone. I heard someone calling my name, and I walked into the thin pine forest toward the voice. It was a male voice, wait—no, it was two voices—both calling my name. 'Ethan . . . Eeeethaaan . . . ' I had to find out who was calling me. The sounds were coming down from the beach, so I headed that way. In no time at all I was standing right there where we had left the canoe earlier, but it was gone now. Instead, wriggling on the sand and gravel of the beach, there were two giant Northern Pikes, like in the pictures in my dad's book. The fish were as big as humans, and then they did something unimaginable. They stood up on their tails, using them as legs!

I wanted to scream, but my mouth went dry. I wanted to run, but my legs wouldn't move—they sank into the sand. And as the giant fish stood up, they turned and fixed their gaze on me. Their eyes were brilliantly green, almost too bright to look at, but I couldn't divert my eyes. As I stood there, my face frozen in horror, the two giant fish started moving towards me, growing arms and hands. Their bright green eyes transformed into bright red flames burning ferociously in their sockets. As they reached out to grab me, their fish heads turned into Jason and Will's faces. Their slimy, newly-grown hands were sliding over my face, leaving gooey traces all over it. Then they started to shake me, and I finally screamed.

8

I opened my eyes, still screaming, and saw Karen's hypnotizing green eyes staring at me in shock. It took me a few moments to shake off the dream, and realize that Karen was there, trying to wake me up. I almost fell out of the hammock while trying to climb out of it, ungracefully, but thankfully I didn't. I'm sure Matt was disappointed with that—he would've laughed his pants off if that had happened. He was already awake, and coming out of the cabin with a glass of water for Karen. *Just pathetic. Sucking up to a girl like that*, I thought.

'Thank you, Matt!' Karen said with a big smile on her face as she took the glass from him. He just nodded. 'Sorry again about earlier, about my cousins. They can really be jerks sometimes.'

'Don't worry about it,' I rushed to stop her apologizing. 'It's not your fault.'

'Still. I'm sorry.' She glanced at both of us, as if

making sure that we knew she really was.

'Anyway, my grandmother sent me over to pick up some books of hers. And then I thought I should tell you a story of my own. Can you guys keep a secret?'

'A secret? What kind of a secret?' I uttered, totally awake by that point.

'A few days ago, I was helping my grandmother clean up the cabin. You know, for arriving guests and all—' She lifted up her glass and took a long sip. I just stared at her, impatiently.

'And then I found something while I was cleaning the study. Later I put it back where I had found it, because I didn't know what it was for. Until—'

She took a deep breath, and looked straight into my eyes.

'Until what?' I pressed.

She put her glass on the small table and said, 'come and take a look at this.'

She led us upstairs, and into the study where we had met her grandmother earlier. I followed in right behind her, and Matt, being the last, slowly closed the door.

'See that little cabinet?' Karen pointed at a small three-drawer wooden cabinet in the left corner. 'I knocked a pen off of it and it fell behind.

When I tilted it, I noticed one of the wooden floor planks was moving. Guess what I found in the hole under that plank?'

I wasn't going to guess. Way ahead of everybody, and always ready for action, I leapt forward, tilted the cabinet, and found the hole under the plank.

'There's a key in here!'

I picked it up, and turned toward Karen and Matt. It didn't look familiar, not like it opened a normal lock. It looked old and special, and felt very cool in my perspiring hand. 'What is it for?' I asked Karen.

'That's the question, isn't it?' She sighed before continuing, clearly knowing more about the key. 'Did my grandmother ever tell you the entire story?'

'What do you mean 'the entire story'? I don't know,' I shook my head. 'What is the entire story?'

'Did she tell you about the story of an old map of the cave system? The story about the Davenport family diamond? The story of the Heart of the Island?'

'No. She skipped *that* part,' Matt chimed in, intrigued.

'Did she now?' Karen smirked. 'Well, my

grandmother and her father had a big fight a long time ago, when she was still very young. Apparently, he had lost a lot of the family's fortune, and possibly the diamond, and she resented him for it. So when he passed away, she didn't really care what happened to his stuff. The only thing she took back to the Lakeview house was an old chest with some of his documents and paperwork. That chest is still in the office room of our Lakeview house—' she paused a beat.

'Ok, and?' I was getting impatient again with the long story. And hot. It was really getting hot up there behind the glass wall.

'And after I'd found that key, I went through that old chest, trying to find anything that would tell me what it's for.'

'So? Did you find anything?' Matt asked before I could.

'I found my great-grandfather's old diary. And I found this in it,' she took a single piece of paper out of her shorts pocket, and straightened it out on the desk.

'What's that?' I asked, leaning in to have a better look. It was a piece of paper, a page torn out of an old notebook or something.

'It's a page from my great-grandfather's diary. Look at that drawing,' she held a finger right over a pencil drawing of a key. The same key I was still holding in my hand. And on the same page below the drawing, there was a hand-written paragraph:

'*I have put the map of the diamond's whereabouts in a safe place. Where the key to that place is hidden, shall remain a secret to all but my family.*'

'So, maybe he hadn't lost the diamond, The Heart of the Island? Maybe he just hid it somewhere,' I said.

'Exactly,' Karen said.

'Wow,' I muttered. 'That's cool. But I still don't see what we can we do about this. I mean, you don't know where that 'safe place' is, right?'

Karen lifted her eyes from the old diary page and looked straight at me. 'Maybe I do.'

9

Matt and I looked at Karen like she'd been hit on the head with something. Our mouths hung wide open, and we stood frozen in time for a long moment there. The sudden silence in the room made all the other noise much clearer. The tireless crickets outside in the trees were louder than ever, and there were a couple of flies buzzing over our heads, right under the light fixture hanging from the ceiling.

'What do you mean, 'maybe I do'?' Matt asked, making a split-second pause before repeating what Karen just said.

'Like I said—maybe I do. In that old chest, the one with my great-grandfather's stuff, there's an old steel safe box.'

'A box?' I interrupted. 'But the diary says a 'place', not a box.'

'True.' She shrugged. 'But a box is also a 'safe place', right? Anyway, I couldn't find the key for it anywhere, and my grandmother said she doesn't have one either. She said she'd looked in that safe years ago, but just found some old papers, so she locked it back up. And now she has no idea where the key is. So I think we should check it out. Maybe this key will open it.'

'Wait, wait— why us?' I asked, and glanced at Matt at the same time. He caught my glance and nodded, obviously thinking the same thing.

'Because I want to find the diamond and return it to my family. Maybe we can reclaim the island for the Davenports again. We were the richest family in the county once, and now I have to put up with these new-money people using the place for their fun—'

'I'm sorry your family is not as rich anymore, but I don't know . . . What's in it for us?' I asked, although I knew Matt and I would end up going. He looked me as if to say, *'What's going on? Let's go!'*

Karen looked a little annoyed now. 'Look, you guys can help me with this or not. Your choice. I'm going back home tomorrow, and I could use some help if I'm going to get to the bottom of this—'

'Ok, ok,' I shrugged and raised my hands apologetically. 'Of course we'll help you—'

'Besides, who else am I gonna ask for help? Jason and Will? They threatened me too, remember? And maybe you can get one over on them if you help me find our family's diamond—that's what's in it for you!' Karen made a good point.

'Ok, so now what? What do we do now? You say the box is in that chest in your house?'

'Yes. So we should go there and see if this key opens it. That's all we can do. Just check it out, that's all.' Karen said.

'But how do we get there? We don't have our bikes here like you do, and I'm not walking all the way to Lakeview in this heat—'

Being a practical girl, and obviously a leader, Karen said we should use our canoe, and I liked that idea. In this heat, just being close to the water would be refreshing, and I was almost hoping Matt would do the same canoe-toppling prank again. So we made quick plans, and she said she'd meet us at the little beach next to the Lakeview dock. She said we could pull the canoe out of the water there, just like everyone else. Then we went outside, and she took the key out of my hand before riding off on her bike towards her house.

***

Not long after that, we were pulling the canoe out of the water at the Lakeview beach. The paddling there was short and boring, I guess because we decided we wanted to be dry for going into Karen's house. While we pulled the canoe out, Karen was already there, waiting for us.

'Just leave it there. Don't worry—this town is too boring for anything as exciting as a boat theft to happen.'

'Any chance we might run into your 'friendly' cousins?' I asked, my eyes darting around, looking for the two bullies.

'Hope not,' she said, 'they're meaner and angrier than ever this summer. I guess it's because they're getting bored here at the lake, or maybe because they've heard people making jokes about our family and the lost wealth . . . So I've got to warn you; they are not harmless—'

'Whoa! Hold on, what do you mean 'not harmless'?' I demanded.

'Well, until this summer they would only tease the newcomers, maybe prank them or something, but this year they've picked it up a notch. Just last week they took a kid in a boat over to the other side of the lake and tied him to a tree. Then they attached a target to his chest and practiced shooting at him with their BB guns. Then they threatened him not to tell anybody who did it, or they would drown him in the lake. The poor kid stayed tied to the tree until the next morning, before he managed to untie himself. He was all battered up and had a hundred mosquito bites on his face alone!'

'That's messed up,' I said, feeling my jaw and my fists clenching in outrage. 'Somebody should do something about them!'

'Probably, but that's not why we're here!' Karen said. 'The house is this way. Come on!'

We followed Karen down the main street leading away from the small dock. As we walked, Karen and I were chatting about all sorts of stuff, like school, hobbies, and of course, our parents. At our age, it was super easy to agree that parents suck. Matt wasn't saying much, as usual.

The street followed the waterline on one side, and on the other side there were small, narrow streets coming down from the houses and small shops sprawled on the surrounding slopes. We turned up one of those streets, and, to our surprise, realized it was no more than a dirt road, with a few houses hiding behind tall hedges and closed gates. I was guessing that either people didn't like their neighbors much in this little town, or they just really appreciated their privacy.

Finally, we stopped in front of a large wooden driveway gate, which had a built-in pedestrian door. Karen stuck her hand behind a large stone flower pot beside the gate, and pulled out the key to the in-built door.

'Your family sure likes to hide keys,' I said, jokingly.

Karen just smiled at the joke, opened the door and said, 'After you, gentlemen.'

10

The house had two stories and was pretty big, with a large porch, and a garage off to the side of the huge front garden. Not bad for basically a summer house, I thought.

'Is your grandma home?' Matt suddenly asked an obvious question.

'No, she went to visit some friends in the town. Probably playing rummy or canasta or some other ancient game. She won't be home until later tonight.'

Then, I could hear it before I could see it, the huff and puff of a large dog, and soon enough, there was a big German Shepherd leaping towards us from behind a corner of the house. He—Karen called him Charlie—was the sweetest dog ever, frolicking around Karen, his tail wagging so hard I thought he might take off!

'Whoa,' I exhaled in relief. 'You could've told us there's a bear-sized dog in here!' My heart was still pounding from surprise like it wanted to burst out of my chest, but Matt was already down on his knees, scratching the dog behind his ears. The dog seemed to really enjoy it, so I joined Matt in petting the jolly beast.

After the dog made sure that we were friends, he went away to attend to his business, and Matt and I followed Karen into the house.

Karen pulled open the screen door and unlocked the front door. We followed her in cautiously, as if we were expecting another surprise, or another set of huge teeth snapping at us. The house looked like any other on the inside, with a large living area and the kitchen off to one side on the ground floor, and a staircase leading upstairs to the bedrooms. We climbed the wooden stairs, and Karen lead the way into a room she called an office, but to me it looked more like a museum, or a library. The room was filled with books, on bookshelves top to bottom, and where there were no books, there were pieces of art—paintings, sculptures, and all sorts of weird-looking objects.

Karen strode over the carpeted floor straight to the back of the room, and put her hand on an old wooden chest. 'This is it,' she said, waiting for Matt and me to gather around.

'It doesn't look like much. It's just a wooden chest,' Matt pointed out, seemingly disappointed with it.

'What did you expect? A shiny golden box or something?' I asked, drawing a chuckle from Karen. 'It does look old—maybe it's a good sign!' I continued, as if I believed in really finding something interesting in that old thing.

Karen glanced at Matt, and then at me. Suddenly she seemed hesitant to continue with our little adventure.

'You ok?' I said. 'Are you sure this is ok? Your grandma won't mind that we were digging through her old stuff if she finds out?'

'Yeah, I'm sure. And besides, it's not *her* old stuff—it belonged to my great-grandfather,' Karen said, confidence back in her voice.

'Did you talk to her at all? Does she know about the key?' Matt was curious.

'No. She would just try to stop me from trying to find out. She is still mad at my great-grandfather, and won't even talk about him. She would just discard anything I said about him— wouldn't even listen.'

'So what do we do if the key really opens the safe?' I still wasn't convinced we should be doing this.

'We look for the map, duh,' Karen said, looking at me as if I were the stupidest guy on Earth.

'Yes, yes, but what if there actually *is* a map? What do we do then?'

'I don't know. It depends what's on it,' Karen said, and with that, swung open the chest top, and we peered inside.

The chest had a couple of file folders and piles of paper stacked to the left side, and on the right, there was a small metal safe box. The safe wasn't modern looking, like with a dial or any buttons— it only had a keyhole and a door handle. Karen took the key out of her pocket, and slowly slid it all the way into the keyhole. The key fit perfectly. She jiggled it in the keyhole a few times before turning it. It seemed to work. She pressed down on the handle to open the door, but it wouldn't budge.

The door handle was stuck.

Karen pulled herself away from the safe box, and I glanced at Matt. He looked as puzzled as I was. *Why won't that door open?* I asked myself, before saying out loud, 'ok, so what are we gonna do now? Matt? Any ideas?'

'Uh, not really,' he shrugged and inspected the safe more closely, trying to find the problem. 'Maybe there's a rubber seal around the door frame or something. Maybe it melted in this heat, I don't know—'

'Wait, what was that?' A faint metallic clanking sound startled me. Something mechanical, a low 'click'—coming from the safe box.

11

'It must be some sort of a time-delay lock,' Karen said. She reached for the handle again, pressed on it, and the door opened all the way this time, very smoothly. All three of us sighed in relief and excitement and shuffled closer together to inspect the box.

Then, instead of looking inside the safe box, our heads turned towards the open window as we heard Charlie barking at the house gate. But that didn't worry me. It was just barking. What I heard after Charlie stopped barking, was much, much worse.

My eyes locked with Karen's, and I saw surprise in them, too. 'If they find us in here, we're dead. Not even you can help us now, we're going to have to fight them!' I whispered, worried that Jason and Will could hear me through the open window.

Karen still looked unsure what to do, and I

saw Matt already looking for good hiding places, calmly, rationally, as only he could have.

'I don't think they'll come in here,' Karen scoffed, disgust on her face, 'there's nothing in here that interests them. Just books.'

I stopped looking for a place to hide and glanced back at her. I was really hoping she was right—I didn't want to be beaten up by some bullies in a strange house. How would I explain that to my parents?

'They probably just came back to get something from the kitchen,' Karen continued. 'They'll be on their way soon.'

I wasn't going to take her word for it, so I tried to make myself as invisible and still as possible behind a curtain. Matt found a place behind a sofa off to the side wall, away from the door. The room went quiet. Each one of my deep breaths sounded like a loud roar in my head. My whole body was sweating while I stood still in that stuffy place between the glass window and the curtain. The smell of the lake water was coming off of me, and I was sure that we'd get caught. Even if they couldn't see me, they could still smell me, that was for sure.

The voices were now inside the house. I could hear Jason and Will, but I couldn't make out what they were saying. I just knew that Karen had been wrong—they were coming straight upstairs.

The door opened, and I held my breath.

'Hey!' Jason said, surprised to see Karen in the room. 'What are you doing—'

'None of your business,' she cut him off. 'And you have no business being here. Nothing for you in here, you should go away!'

I was amazed with Karen's courage. I mean, they were cousins, so I figured that they wouldn't really hurt her, but still. She was very brave, and she was trying to get them out of that room to save our behinds.

'But—' Jason started, but was cut off again by Karen's stern voice. Maybe she was just drawing courage from the fact that we were in their grandmother's house. Maybe this was safe ground.

'I said, right now. You should really get out of here—right now,' she said very calmly, slowly, like she was trying to hypnotize them.

'Oh. Oh, ok—we'll go now,' Will suddenly said, as if he'd just thought of something else they needed to do, or someplace else they needed to be. I wasn't sure Karen would be safe once she left the house—there was something in Will's voice when he said they would go.

They closed the door, and walked down the stairs. I listened to them opening the front door and leaving the house. They were chuckling and talking quietly to each other, all the way to the gate. I was sure they were making some horrible plans how to get back at Karen. I was also grateful that they had missed the fact that Matt and I were in the room, hiding in their own house.

When the house and the yard got quiet again, I stepped out from behind the curtain, and saw Matt already stretching his legs and his back beside the sofa. He'd been crouched right there on the floor behind it the whole time. He nodded gratefully at Karen, and I said 'thanks', feeling bad that we'd gotten her in trouble with her cousins.

The three of us then shuffled towards the old chest. The safe box inside it was still open, it's secrets waiting to be discovered.

Matt and I pulled the old safe box out of the chest, and set it down on the floor next to it. It was made of steel, I thought, but the steel was thin and not too heavy, so we pulled it out to get a better look.

12

Karen opened the door again, and we all peered inside. There was only one shelf in it, right in the middle of the box, with some old documents and unsealed envelopes piled on top of it. I took the envelopes and started flipping through them and opening them, finding nothing that looked like a map in the process.

'No map here,' I said, looking into the last of the envelopes. Matt and Karen were browsing through the sheets of paper, finding nothing as well. Matt glanced at me, and shrugged his shoulders.

We put everything back on the shelf, and turned our focus to the bottom of the box. Again, some old documents, some old medical bills and a small collection of old silver dollars, probably not worth very much.

Nothing there, either.

The disappointment sagged our bodies and we

just sat there, very still. It felt like the whole room exhaled and sighed at the same time. *Great*, I thought. *I just love it when I get overexcited about something, and then nothing happens*.

'Ok, so we almost got beat up in this house for nothing,' I said, annoyed with the lack of any result. I realized I was really hoping to find something. 'We should put everything back in, and leave it where it was. Or you do whatever you want with it, I wanna get out of here now, and go back to the beach!' I said, regretting the way it sounded. I wasn't really mad at Karen, I was just disappointed.

'Sorry, I thought—' Karen mumbled.

'I'm sorry. Not your fault. I just really wanted to find something,' I cut her off and apologized. It really wasn't her fault, it was mine and Matt's curiosity that brought us here, not Karen. She didn't exactly have to twist our arms to get us here, now did she?

But I wanted to get out of there—I didn't want to be grounded for the rest of my life because of some old story! My mom still hadn't called us, but I had the feeling she might. And if she knew we were doing this, she would have been furious. There would be no explaining why we'd been sneaking around in someone else's home, going through their safe box. She wouldn't even care.

'I really wish I could find the cursed thing. My diamond. First thing I'd do is close that horrible hotel on my island . . . ' Karen muttered under her breath, and started returning the rest of the stuff back into the box. As she put the small silver dollar collection in, she suddenly paused.

'Wait a minute—' She glanced back toward Matt and me. 'The bottom of this box . . . It moves!' She said, excitement rising in her voice.

'What do you mean?' Matt went down to take a closer look.

'I mean, it moves. Only slightly, but look—' she put her fingers on top of what looked like a plywood bottom plate and jiggled it. It was definitely moving. Like it could be lifted and taken out. Like there could be something under it—a piece of paper, maybe? A map, maybe?

'Hand me that letter opener, will you?' Karen said, and nodded at the work desk without even glancing at me. On the desk, there was a square wooden pen holder, with a few pens in, and an old-fashioned metal letter opener.

'Sure.' I knew what she was about to try. I stood up from crouching behind her and Matt and got the letter opener. Handed it to her, and crouched right back behind them.

She took it from my hand and jammed it straight between the plywood plate and the metal bottom of the safe box. She pressed down on the letter opener, using it as a lever. As it jammed itself under the plywood plate, the plate popped up, and she grabbed it. She pulled the thin square piece of plywood out, and we all stared at a folded sheet of paper at the bottom of the safe box.

13

Karen stood there, triumphantly, her chin up, her eyes locked on mine, as if to say 'Told you so'. But she didn't. I thought her manners were better than mine—I would've said that for sure. And maybe more. Maybe I'd have done a little victory dance and gloated annoyingly. Well, I wouldn't think it's annoying. That's why, in the end, I thought it a good thing that it was her who'd found the map, not me. For the sake of friendship, you see.

And yes, it was a map. I knew it even before Matt gently removed it from its hideout at the bottom of that metal box and handed it to me. Then I placed it on the desk, and, even more gently, slowly unfolded it, holding the paper with only my thumbs and my index fingers.

The paper looked old and yellowish. On the left side, there was a crude drawing of an island, which Karen recognized as Dead-end Island itself. On the right, there was some sort of a weird shape, like an outline of an ink blob, not making much sense to me at the first glance.

'What is that'? I asked, pointing my finger at the blob.

'It's the caves. What did you think it was'? Karen said, but not expecting me to reply. 'The big open space in the middle is called the 'Main Hall', and you can see how all the tunnels lead away from it, but stop at dead ends.'

'Ah, I get it now!' The drawing suddenly made a whole lot more sense to me. 'And these tunnels here? This looks like a maze!' I was drawing a circle in the air over parts of the map with my finger now.

'Yeah, some of these tunnels widen into rooms, and some of these rooms have more than one tunnel leading in and out. And some tunnels just circle straight back into the same rooms they've started from, so yes, it really is a maze. It used to be really dangerous down there, before the caves were totally explored.'

I wasn't convinced. I mean, *used to be dangerous*'? As in, *'not anymore'*? Really? But I wanted to know more, so I said, 'Sure. Doesn't sound dangerous at all. Have you been there before'?

'Yes. A few times, actually. It's not too difficult to get around now, since the caves have been mapped out. But imagine being there, wandering around in the dark, without a map, not knowing where the next turn will take you?'

I shuddered at the thought. I wasn't a huge fan of enclosed spaces—sometimes I'd get nervous even going on a subway train. The idea of getting lost in a cave didn't seem fun to me—not at all. But then she said something that made the hairs on the back of my neck stand up even more.

She said, 'And this room,'—she pointed with her index finger—'is called 'The Nursery'. That's where the bats raise their—'

'Whoa! Bats?! What bats? There are bats in that cave?!' I almost screamed. Did I mention I wasn't a huge fan of bats?

Karen laughed my interruption away and just waved her hand at me.

'Don't be such a baby, the bats won't hurt you. They only stay in this room, the Nursery'—she pointed to a room not far from the Main Hall— 'because it's the warmest, or so I've been told.'

'Well, I'm not sure I want to trust you on that. I hate bats!' I cried.

And I would've kept ranting about them, but then, cool as ever, Matt finally moved. Honestly, he was so quiet and focused on the map, I'd almost forgotten he was there with us.

'There's something here. Move, let me see,' he said, and squeezed past me to get closer to the map. While I was panicking about the bats that I hadn't even seen yet, he had studied the map, and all the tunnels and rooms in the cave.

'You guys see this?' He pointed at a small doodle, so small it could have been mistaken for a smudge.

I looked closer, and straight away, my fear of bats was replaced with something more powerful. Excitement. Lots of it. Euphoria even. I felt butterflies in my stomach and my hands grasped the edge of the table in case my knees gave out. Air got stuck in my throat, and I swallowed hard. Could this be possible?

The doodle was a tiny sketch, and was drawn in a tunnel leading past the entrance to the Nursery. It was a tiny sketch of a diamond.

14

Plans were made quickly. No time to waste, and nobody wanted to—the excitement was too big. Huge, in fact—it's not every day you find an actual treasure map, and you can actually do something about it. Or at least try, of course, nobody guaranteed the map was real, or that the diamond was still there. But we were going to find out, and nothing would stop us.

Matt's eyes were darting left and right as he talked about what to do. He was excited, maybe even more than I was. That was new, I thought.

He said, 'Ok, so we go back to the cabin now, and then meet at the beach later, right? At our canoe, ok?'

'Ok.' Karen and I nodded.

'At midnight?'

'Ok.' I nodded.

'Why so late?' Karen asked.

'We need to make sure Ethan's mom and dad

are asleep.'

'Ok. My grandma goes to bed much earlier, but that's ok. She'll be asleep too.'

'Ok.' Matt and I nodded.

'Ok. Bring a flashlight,' Karen said. 'Text me if anything changes!' she said as she scribbled her number on a piece of paper and handed it to me.

And that was all there was to our planning.

I knew my dad was supposed to get up around four in the morning to go fishing, but I was sure we'd get back by then. Starting our little adventure at midnight sounded cool, but more than that, we were hoping that we wouldn't be seen at that hour. Also—it sounded cool.

We got back to the cabin, and spent the rest of the late afternoon just hanging out, helping Dad organize his fishing rods and bait. At dinner, Mom noticed we—and by 'we' she meant me— behaved unusually well. So I made some bread balls and threw them at Matt, just to make Mom less suspicious. It worked. We might be able to pull off this whole sneaking out business after all.

'Ethan, stop that! What are you, five?!' Mom scolded me, turned to Matt and said, 'Matt, how's the food?' Big smile, her eyes practically melting. She really loved him. Honestly, sometimes I think she'd give me up for him in a heartbeat.

'It's great!' He managed a smile and mumbled with his mouth full.

I wanted to kick him in the shin under the table, but I didn't want to push my luck. We could get grounded tomorrow, or any other day, but not now. Not tonight. So we finished dinner, washed the dishes and parked ourselves in front of the TV to watch a movie. Soon, Mom and Dad said good night and went to their room, but I knew they would still be doing some reading or whatnot. So we still had a couple of hours to kill, and I couldn't wait for that time to pass.

***

Ten minutes before midnight, we were all 'packed' and ready to go. Matt had a small pocket knife, and I was carrying a flashlight. I felt proud of myself for actually checking if the batteries were ok.

The night air felt humid and cool, much cooler than during the day, so we had our hoodies on when we silently crept out of the cabin, and carefully closed the front door behind us. There was some moonlight in the sky, and our eyes were already used to darkness, so there was no need to turn on the flashlight as we strode down to the beach.

The woods were quiet. Nothing but an occasional hoot here and there, and the rustling sound of dry pine needles beneath our feet. There was no chatting going on as we followed the narrow pathway through the trees. I could almost hear the butterflies going crazy inside my belly, and I could tell Matt was psyched too. Were we really about to do this?

We saw Karen's bike leaning against the tree closest to the beach before we actually saw her. A few quiet strides later we found her by the canoe, her phone in her hand, gleaming in the dark.

'Don't have to check for texts—we're here!' I whispered, but it sounded deafening so close to the water.

'Shhhh—keep your voices down!' She put her finger to her mouth and slid her phone into her pocket.

'Did you bring the map?' I blurted, totally unnecessarily. She rolled her eyes and looked at me as if I'd lost my mind. Even Matt raised his palms up and tilted his head quizzically.

'All right, all right, just checking . . . geez, don't kill me, please . . . '

Rather than asking more silly questions, I grabbed one end of the canoe and waited for Matt to grab the other. We put it in the water gently, took off our hoodies, and sat down in the canoe. We'd already put our sneakers in, and I didn't want the hoodie to be all wet and sweaty by the time we got there. Matt was at the back, Karen in the middle, and we started paddling on the dark lake towards the island. We couldn't have imagined how different things would be the next time we saw that beach.

15

The paddles made almost no noise going into the water as Matt and I worked them to propel and steer the canoe. We were paddling in quiet darkness, but the faint moonlight felt brighter on the dark water of the lake than it did on the beach. The island seemed to be further away than it had been earlier that day. I thought it was because of the thin mist that had crept over the lake and reduced visibility. Which actually worked well for us—less chance of being spotted by security, if there was any.

Still, I could make out the outline of the big house, and I could see the small dock. The mansion was bathed in small floodlights scattered around it, just a few at the corners of the buildings, and the lights gave the whole island an eerie appearance. It looked awake, and ready for us.

'Karen, you sure you know your way around

these caves? Your grandma was really serious when she told us not to go in,' I whispered from the front of the canoe.

'Yes, don't worry. I've explored them with Jason and Will many times. They got so obsessed with the story about the diamond, and they started believing they're the only ones that deserve to find the Heart. Or even look for it.'

'Is that why they hate everybody?' Matt muttered from the back.

'Yes. They hate anybody that even thinks about exploring the island or the caves. They're convinced the diamond is still there, and they worry someone will find it by chance.'

'Like us, maybe . . . You think the security guy will still be on the island?' I asked Karen, assuming she might know something we didn't.

'Yes. But I wouldn't worry about him. He's probably sleeping or watching TV somewhere. Nothing ever happens here at night.'

'Hope so . . . Look guys, we're getting close!' I started to steer the canoe away from the now clearly visible small dock we'd seen earlier and the small sandy beach to the left of it.

After just a few strokes, Karen whispered from the middle of the canoe, 'hey, where are you going?'

'Over there,' I pointed with my paddle to the left of the island. 'Around the island to the cave entrance. That's where we're going, right?'

'Wrong,' she said. 'Didn't I tell you? There's another, smaller entrance, just behind the service buildings. But it's easier to get to from the dock, and it's easier to pull the canoe out of the water here.'

'Well, no, you didn't tell us. You had the map the entire time, remember? But never mind, let's just get this thing out of the water and get this over with. I hope the guard is really asleep like you say.'

'Why did they build that main entrance then?' Matt asked from the back. A good question, I thought.

'Because it's wider and easier to walk through into and out of the cave. The one we're going to use is more like a manhole with some ladders. Too difficult for movie stars to climb down, I guess. But it's also closer to the tunnel we're looking for.' Then she stopped talking, and we just paddled in silence, softly, sweating lightly in the cool air.

When we reached the beach, I stepped out of the canoe into the water, and held it steady for Karen and Matt to get out. We half pulled and half carried the canoe out onto the sandy beach, and then took our stuff out. Karen had brought a small towel with her, along with a flashlight of her own, so we didn't have to put our sneakers on wet feet. I was very impressed—that was some smart thinking.

There was no sign of the security guy, but his boat was there, so we carried the canoe and hid it under the small wooden dock anyway. Just in case the guy decided to check the beach while we were sneaking around the island.

Using the dock as our shield, all three of us peered around at the island, trying to see as much as we could. Nothing was moving. Nothing at all—no sign of any security, anybody walking around the island.

I was gazing at the dark pathway around the island, when I realized something—'I think the security guy would carry a flashlight around, right? We'd be able to see the light beam from like, a mile away!'—I whispered.

'True. Let's go,' Matt said, and we all stood up slowly and started creeping up the beach, and onto the pathway toward the service buildings.

As we were about to leave the beach behind us, I turned one last time to check on the canoe and the beach. I thought I could make out our footsteps in the sand, but just because I knew they were there. No way to see them unless you were really looking for them, so I wasn't too worried. I turned my head back to Matt and Karen, satisfied. *We might actually be able to pull this off*, I thought.

***

If we'd have turned around, we would have seen a canoe appeared from the now thickening mist over the lake. Jason and Will's eyes shone brightly, reflecting the dim lights coming off the island. Their faces wore a sinister grin, and they weren't making a sound. They paddled gently . . . stroke left . . . paddle out . . . switch side . . . stroke right . . . , quietly . . . no hurry at all—they knew they had plenty of time.

16

The mansion that was now a hotel stood right in front of us, up a short stone-paved walkway coming directly from the dock. The big windows were now dark, and the revolving front door looked locked and stuck in place. There was a small roundabout in front of the revolving door with some kind of a small statue in the center. Probably a fountain as well, but the water wasn't running. There were flowers in the flower beds all around the house, and all along the walkway coming from the dock. The whole thing looked really fancy. Like there would normally be a uniformed doorman, and bellhops waiting to help you to your luxurious rooms. There were a couple of white golf carts parked at one side of the roundabout, obviously being used just to haul rich people's luggage up from the dock. Maybe the rich and famous people themselves— how lazy would that be?!

But I wasn't interested in the mansion all that much, and I guessed neither were Matt and Karen. We had more important things to do, and we shuffled along the pathway in the other direction, towards the service buildings. We were treading lightly, as we didn't want to turn on our flashlights. No point getting almost all the way to the cave, and then announce it to everyone that may be on the island by shining a light in the dark night. We took a small trail branching away from the pathway, and arrived to the paved helipad between the mansion and the service buildings.

The concrete of the helipad suddenly felt good under my feet. Quiet, much quieter than the gravel of the pathway and the small trail. A bright yellow circle was drawn around it, with a big 'H' in the middle—surely clearly visible through the cabin window of a landing helicopter. The pile of old furniture looked even bigger from up close, but I noticed now that it was neatly stacked in rows, not just piled up like it seemed to have been from the water level. We trudged onwards, along one of the rows, our dry sneakers making no sound at all on the hard surface. So at first, I was confused when I heard the crunching of the gravel.

The sound brought us all to a dead stop. We turned our heads toward the source—the gravel pathway we'd been following until a minute ago. Then I saw a narrow light beam, bouncing over the gravel pathway and the hedge roots. The security guy held a small flashlight, walking unhurriedly, returning to the mansion from the other side of the island. He didn't seem alarmed, and more importantly—he didn't seem to have noticed us. I could tell because there was no yelling, no 'who are you' and 'stop right there' shouting, and the light beam stayed away from us. We could see him clearly now, and his footsteps grew louder. The man wore some kind of a uniform, like security guards at a mall, and a baseball cap on his head, with 'Security' inscribed on the front.

As if we had somehow heard each others' thoughts, without saying a word, Matt, Karen and I cautiously tiptoed back behind the closest row of the old furniture. Once out of sight behind an old broken desk, I started breathing again. We looked at each other, and shrugged. What now? Nothing to be done—we just had to wait for him to go away. No talking necessary.

I felt safe enough to start gazing around— it looked like the guy would just finish his rounds and go back to the main building. But I couldn't see much, other than the old furniture. It looked expensive, but worn out, like it had seen better days. The desk we were hiding behind had cabinets on both sides, but both had been shattered when they dumped the desk there. The cabinet drawers were spilled open, and there was some stuff lying around on the concrete floor. I was being very careful not to touch anything—not to make any noise—so I stared open-mouthed at Matt when I saw him pick through the small pile of, it seemed, ancient leather-bound notebooks, some leather pouches and small cardboard boxes.

I brought my finger to my lips to remind him that we needed to be quiet, and not explore every little thing that we find interesting along the way. He glanced at me innocently and nodded that he understood. But I could see he was still interested in that pile of old stuff. I turned to Karen and rolled my eyes at her, but she just grinned. I guess we all felt a bit safer, with the security guy almost out of sight. I could still see the glow of his flashlight, and it was moving steadily toward the mansion.

'Phew,' I whispered, turning to Karen again. 'That was close!'

Karen made a deep sigh of relief and agreed,

'Yeah. Let's hope now he stays glued to his TV for the rest of the night.'

I heard Matt shuffling behind me, still going through the stuff scattered around the broken cabinet. 'You ok back there? Checked everything out? Can we get going now?' I muttered.

'Yeah, but check this out; these notebooks belonged to someone called Jacob Davenport. Karen, do you know who that was?'

Karen's eyes turned to Matt as she quickly shuffled towards him, 'Yes, that was my grandmother's dad. The guy who lost my diamond! Let me see that, maybe we can find out more.'

'*My diamond*'? *I guess Jason and Will were not the only ones obsessing about it*, I thought.

But we couldn't find out more. It was too dark to read, and we didn't want to risk turning on our flashlights. So we put some of that stuff in our pockets to check out later, got up and took a long look around to make sure the security guy was gone. Once we were satisfied, we jogged to the service buildings, and went around behind them. A short grassy path led to the entrance from the service building. The path was dewy and slippery, slightly inclined, so we all slipped a few times and had to break our fall with our hands. I figured that I'd get myself even more dirty in that cave so I didn't think too much about it.

There, just a few steps from a large trash dumpster, was a big rocky hole in the ground. Not really concealed, but clearly not used very often, either. I stared at the dark mouth of the hole, noticing the iron bars serving as ladders drilled into the side of it. I took a deep breath, and glanced at Matt. He looked just as nervous as I was.

17

I stared at the shaft in the ground that looked like a manhole, only without the round metal lid on top.

Karen stepped up to the rocky edge of the shaft, sat on it and her feet found an iron ladder bar lower down in the hole.

She glanced up at us and said, 'You guys coming or what?'

I liked her courage. If I hadn't seen her go down that hole so bravely, I'm not sure I'd have been able to do it myself. Maybe Matt would have forced me to do it—otherwise I'd never hear the end of it.

Karen grasped the ladder bar at the top and descended down the hole. A few seconds later, she'd already reached the bottom of the shaft, and Matt and I could see the reassuring glow of Karen's flashlight gleaming from down below.

'After you, sir,' I said to Matt with a fake

comical expression on my face. Standing out there, watching Karen descend below ground made all this suddenly seem very real. *What are we doing here? Have we lost our minds?*!

My heart was fluttering in my chest and my palms were very sweaty. I hoped I wouldn't lose grip on the iron ladder bars and fall down that shaft. As funny as it would have been for Matt—not Karen, I hoped—it would be very painful, that's for sure. So I 'manned up', whatever that meant, wiped my hands dry on my shirt, and followed Matt down the shaft and into the cave.

Once underground, I turned on my flashlight, and Karen led the way down the narrow tunnel, towards the Main Hall. I shuffled along at the back of our little column, holding the flashlight in my right hand, trying to keep the beam of light steady on the right-hand wall. The floor of the cave was pure rock, as were most of the walls and the ceiling. The rock felt cool and slippery, but the air in the tunnel was thick and warm. Our walking made an echoing noise, and I kept turning my head back around to make sure there was nobody following us.

Matt broke the silence first. 'Can I have the map for a sec?' he asked Karen.She handed him the map and we moved on. The tunnel started to widen a little, and I could feel the air move on my face, only slightly, but enough to feel that we were about to come to a large, open space. Karen's light beam suddenly extended into the darkness, much wider at the end. Matt moved to her side, and I stepped to his. We had reached the Main Hall.

I tried to look around, aiming my flashlight left and right, but it was pointless. The light was nowhere near strong enough to penetrate the deep darkness of the cave, and everything looked exactly the same. Rock, rock, and more rock. I could only make out the large open space in the middle, slightly inclining toward the far side, and a few tunnels leading away from the large room. It was only when I shone my light at the tunnels that I saw the barred gates at the end of each one. The gates were wide open, leaning on the walls of the Main Hall, but it was obvious they were there to prevent access to the tunnels.

'What are those gates for?' I asked Karen, pointing my beam toward the closest gate.

'To keep the tourists out when the bats are here for the winter,' she said. 'They come in huge numbers, so people are only allowed to look around the Main Hall, not down the tunnels. I mean, there are still bats in the Nursery now, but not as many. In the winter, there's tens of thousands of them in there! And the barred gates let them fly in and out whenever they want.'

I pondered on the idea of tens of thousands of those nasty, pointy-toothed, flying rats, and my whole body shuddered. Still, it could be worse. We could have been doing this in the winter, right?

Matt held the map up and motioned to Karen to give him some light. Karen aimed her flashlight, and we all stared down at it to figure out where to go next.

'Ok, so I think we need to take the third tunnel to the right, right?' he said.

Karen looked down at the map and confirmed, 'Yes. I think it shouldn't be too far, at least that's what the map says.' She aimed her flashlight at the wall to our right, and then swept the light beam slowly over it, counting the tunnels, 'one . . . two . . . three! It should be that one.'

The tunnel waited there, maybe fifty, sixty feet away, shadows playing a freakish game on its walls when we pointed our two flashlights at it. No turning back now, so we started walking straight across the Main Hall, and into the tunnel.

18

The tunnel was slightly wider and a little taller than the one we used to get down from the cave entrance. Karen was leading the way, confidently, even without the map. I was at the rear again, occasionally checking the map in Matt's hands, but there wasn't much need for that. We were in the right tunnel, according to the map, and not too far from the place that was marked with a tiny diamond sketch on it.

As we were passing a small corridor on our left-hand side, my nose wrinkled in disgust. A foul stench was coming out of that tunnel, and I could also feel, rather than hear, some fluttering commotion in there. Like some sort of vibrating sensation in the still air of the cave.

'What's that smell?' I asked, but knowing the answer already.

'It's the Nursery. I told you about it—it's the only room where the bats stay and breed in the winter, and it smells bad, yes. There's a lot of bat poop in there, you know,' Karen explained.

Knowing the answer didn't make the fact that there were bats just down that short little corridor any better. My stomach still churned from that awful, foul-smelling stench. The hairs on the back of my neck stood on end and I urged Karen and Matt to move on, so we trudged along the more-or-less straight tunnel. The damp air still smelled bad a minute further down the tunnel, when Karen stopped to take a look at the map in Matt's hands.

'I think this is it. This is where the diamond is supposed to be,' she said, and started gazing at the walls around her. 'Come on, let's see if we can find anything, then let's get out of here!'

'You sure this is the spot?' I asked, and studied the map.

'Looks like it,' Matt said, his finger pointing directly at the tiny diamond sketch on the map. The map was getting all dirty and had mud and grime from our hands all over it. I figured that wouldn't be a problem, since the only way out for us from this spot would be straight back down the tunnel and out of the cave. Piece of cake.

Matt put the map in his pocket, and we started

turning our heads in every possible direction. I realized suddenly that I'd forgotten about the dark, the bad smell, and about the bats. I didn't care about anything other than finding that diamond. But I didn't know where to look. The light beam coming out of my flashlight jumped wildly up and down the walls of the tunnel, even up on the ceiling and over the rock floor. Karen looked puzzled, not really sure where to point the beam either.

'Guys, we need to calm down and think,' Matt said in the dark, and flinched away as I blasted his eyes with the light, accidentally. 'We need to figure out a system or something.'

I nodded in the dark. He was right, and I was really glad he was there. He was sometimes really annoyingly calm and robot-like, but it wasn't bothering me now. Not down there in the cave tunnels. There, he was a rock to lean on. There is a reason why we're best friends.

'Ok, but what kind of system?' I asked. 'Like each one of us takes a wall or something and looks only at that?'

'Yeah—something like that. I'll take this wall'

So he took out his phone, and used the small flashlight to explore the left-hand-side wall. Or right-hand side—it depends on the way you look at it, I guess. I took the other wall, and Karen started swiping the rock floor with a beam of light. Nothing there. Nothing anywhere.

'I knew this was some kind of a diabolical joke. Now I understand why Grandma didn't like her father,' Karen muttered, but we could hear it clearly in the gloomy, hushed tunnel. 'You really can't trust the Davenport family . . . ' She said, with a wistful sigh.

I didn't blame her. It was not her fault we hadn't found anything, and besides, Matt and I were just as excited to explore as she was. I didn't know what to do at that point, so I just stared at my wall, hoping something would reveal itself, some hint or a clue showing where the diamond might be.

Then I had an idea. Not a great one, but at least it felt like I was still trying. So I said, 'Why don't we rotate? I mean, I'll check out the floor now, Karen should check out your wall, and you can check my wall,' I said, explaining the idea to Matt as he stood right next to me. We shuffled around to start the search again, when the silence of the cave was abruptly broken. Jason and Will's voices were unmistakable. What wasn't really clear to me was where they were coming from—the voices seemed to echo in from both directions of the tunnel, even from the ceiling.

The cousins were obviously having a blast, taunting us in unison in annoyingly mocking, singsongy voices—'Hey guys . . . Remember us?'

19

I don't know why exactly, but a second after we heard the horrifying echo I turned off my flashlight. Maybe I thought that we could hide in the dark, like somehow they wouldn't know where to look for us, but that was obviously just wishful thinking. They knew where we were—they were just toying with us. Besides, Karen still kept her flashlight turned on, and was now aiming her beam right down the tunnel the way we came from.

'How did they get here?!' Matt cried.

I guess I was still too shocked, because it would normally be me to speak first out of the two of us.

'Never mind that—what do they want?' It was my turn to be calm and rational now.

'I think we all know what they want, and how they got here—they were following me from the house! They must've suspected that I'd found out something about the diamond. Don't worry guys,

I won't let them hurt you!' Karen said, resolve in her voice.

Loud, eerie, ghostly laughter bounced off of the walls and the ceiling and the floor. Still sounded like only Jason and Will, but the voices seemed to have been multiplied in the tunnels, and they roared in the air all around me. The walls seemed to have closed in a bit. The tunnel seemed narrower and the air seemed cooler. I shuddered, wildly turning my head toward one end of the tunnel, then the other. I fully expected to see them both come charging at us at any moment, and I was bracing myself for it, holding onto the wall, my knees rattling like a dashboard doll. My hands, although pressed against the cool rock, were soaked with sweat. I glanced at Matt. I knew he was just as terrified, but he wasn't showing it. He was keeping his cool.

'Now what?' I said. 'Where do we go?'

'No idea. They could be anywhere!' Matt replied, his voice cracking a bit.

At that point, Karen let out a high-pitched howl, 'Leave us alone!'

I thought she finally felt scared like Matt and I. The screaming was pointless and an act of panic, and it could have led them straight to us, if they had doubts about our location at all. After a short delay, their response came echoing through the tunnel, no way of knowing where from, exactly.

'That can be arranged!' They sang, followed with roaring belly laughter. They were really having a great time. Jerks.

I hoped that Karen would be able to save us once again, but hearing the two cousins laughing like that made me think she wouldn't. And all of this over nothing. So I started preparing myself to fight back, as much as I could, and I knew Matt was doing the same. We were not cowards, but I knew we probably couldn't win a fight against them, if it came to that.

My mental rollercoaster was suddenly interrupted when Karen tripped clumsily over a bump on the rocky floor. She started plummeting to the floor, but managed to catch herself in a push-up position, like a cat. Impressive.

She composed herself for a long moment, reaching for and grabbing the flashlight that had fallen out of her hand. As she turned the flashlight to pick it up, the beam of light shone over the floor, and toward the wall, revealing a small crack at the bottom. She lowered her head and set it flat down on the rocky floor, peered into the illuminated crack, and said, 'Wait a minute—there's something down here.'

20

Funny how you can forget the danger when something really excites you. When you just have to know what's out there, what happens next. Maybe it was just that we knew we were going to have to deal with Jason and Will one way or the other—but at least it wouldn't all be for nothing. Or at least that was what I was hoping for.

So both me and Matt threw ourselves down next to Karen. I laid down on the cold and moist rock floor, my head flat against it, and I pointed my flashlight into the small crack at the base of the wall. The crack was small and well concealed from anybody standing up and looking down at the wall. In the dark of the cave, a flashlight, used while standing up, created an illusion that there was nothing but the floor at the base of the wall.

'Whoa. You see that?' I asked no-one in particular.

'Looks like a box. A metal box.' Matt said.

'Can you reach it?' Karen glanced at me, as I was the closest to it.

I gave my flashlight to Matt to keep the light beam pointed into the crack, and I went for it.

'I hope there aren't any rats, or scorpions, or whatever in there,' I muttered, groping around, my fingers reaching out and trying to grab the small box. I couldn't see inside the crack anymore, as I had to lift my head up to push my arm all the way in. The sleeves of my hoodie were getting stuck in the tight crack, so I pulled out my hand, rolled the sleeve up, and went for it again. I pushed my arm in, extending it from my shoulder as much as I could. Grabbing the rocky floor with my fingers to help it along. Big drops of sweat formed on my forehead, and I held my breath, reaching for the box. *C'mon, just a little more . . .*

'Got it!' I exhaled. I pulled my arm out of the crack, holding onto the prize with just my thumb and my index finger. Matt and Karen were already standing up, so I got up to my feet, and opened my hand in front of them. I had a few scratches on my lower arm, but I couldn't care less about it at that moment. I was holding a small metal box in my hand, rattling quietly every time it moved, obviously hiding something hard inside.

'Well? Open it. Let's see what's in it!' Karen urged me.

As if to amplify the urgency in Karen's voice, Will started singing again—to Jason's amusement, as he snickered loudly—'Yoo-hoo . . . Where are you . . . ?'

I didn't want to waste any more time, so I handed the flashlight to Matt, and he aimed it straight at the little box. I opened the box and gasped.

'Whoa! Is this thing real?'

Matt touched it gently, brushing it with his finger, like he wanted to make sure it wasn't just an illusion or something. 'It looks real,' he said.

'I guess my grandma was wrong. There is something on this island after all!' Karen said, gazing at us, grinning, enjoying the moment.

In the box, there was a diamond. Incredibly shiny in the darkness, reflecting the light beams of the two flashlights into a billion shimmering sparks. A small rainbow appeared on the wall in front of us, showing all colors on the spectrum, quivering as my hand did. It was as big as an egg, its edges perfectly straight and sharp, as if you could cut yourself if not careful.

'We're coming to get you!' Now Jason and Will sang in unison again.

Maybe it was the fear, or the excitement, but the voices sounded a bit closer now, and clearer, like the echo was gone.

All of a sudden, before Matt or I could talk her out of it, Karen turned to us and said, 'Stay here, I'll go check the way we came in!' She ran down the tunnel toward the Main Hall, the light from her flashlight bouncing on the walls as she ran down the tunnel. She turned around a corner, and we could only see the gleam of her light.

Matt and I stood there for a long moment, not sure what to do. We squirmed in place, glancing at each other, turning one ear down the tunnel at a time to try to hear better. Should we go after her? Should we just wait? The realization that we're still trapped in a dark cave with a couple of big guys who wanted to hurt us crept back in. I put the diamond into the pocket on my hoodie, pulled the zipper and slowly put the metal box on the floor. I thought we won't be needing that anymore, and I had no idea what we were going to do with the diamond, but I wanted to make sure we held onto it until we did.

Right about the time it should have taken Karen to reach the Main Hall, we heard a shrill, piercing scream blasting toward us up the tunnel.

'No! Let go of me!' Karen cried, and the next thing we heard was the loud clang of the tunnel's barred gates slamming shut at the Main Hall.

21

'Was that . . . ?' I swallowed hard. My eyes were wide open, and suddenly I was again very aware of the bad smell, of the silent darkness, of the thick air and the moist rock walls.

'Yeah. The gate.' Matt simply stated.

I couldn't be sure whether or not the gate was locked, but I wasn't fooling myself either. Of course they'd locked it—there was no other reason to close those gates. And what about Karen? What were they going to do with her? Are they coming in here, up the tunnel, or did they just lock us in here? All these questions were popping in my head, and I didn't have an answer for them. Matt just stood there, staring at the darkness of the tunnel, probably thinking about the same questions as me.

'What do we do now? We run, or we try to go help her?' I said.

'I don't know where to run to. I think we

should at least see what's going on.'

He was right. I said, 'Yeah. We should. Enough is enough—let's get this over with. Let's go out there and face whatever it is we need to face. Maybe Karen didn't tell them about the diamond, so we can still come out of this like winners!'

Matt nodded, and we headed down the tunnel, looking much more confident than we actually felt. I could tell that even Matt was scared, by the way both of us were slowly shuffling along, stopping to listen ahead often. No sounds coming from the tunnel entrance. No light either, as we passed the Nursery tunnel on our way down the main tunnel. We crept along. One short step at a time, my flashlight illuminating the dark tunnel ahead. As we turned the last corner, the beam of light from my flashlight drew a net-like shadow on the far wall of the Main Hall.

The barred gate was closed, and a few steps behind it, Jason turned his big camping light on and set it on the floor. He was tossing something up in the air and then catching it again, like a weird single-object juggle. His wore a smug grin on his face, obviously very pleased with himself.

I stepped to the gate and tried to open it, but it was locked with a brand new, big padlock. I took another look at Jason and recognized the object he was playing with—a small metal key. I summoned all of my courage, and said, 'Come on man, this isn't funny. Where's Karen? What did you do with her?'

Jason just chuckled and put the key in his pocket. His hand came out of the pocket with a phone, and he started taking a video of me and Matt behind the locked bars. It gave me a desperate idea, but as I took my phone out I knew it wouldn't have any signal, even before I looked at it.

'Good luck finding a signal down here,' Jason taunted us. 'Maybe you can take a video of yourselves for our viewing pleasure later!'

'Let us out of here! Are you crazy?! My mom will kill you when she finds out!' I cried.

The grin on Jason's face turned into a mean frown as he said, 'No she won't. And neither will your dad—and you know why? Because they won't believe you, and we would just deny it anyway. Or maybe you could still get hurt, if you try telling them. They'll both be mad enough because you sneaked out in the middle of the night to go wandering around a cave, and you'll be the ones in trouble.' He let out a sudden laugh, 'A perfect crime, right?'

'But you can't just leave us locked up down here, we could die!'

'Come on . . . Don't be such a drama queen. You'll only spend the night here, that's all. Unless you're brave enough to take the passage through the Nursery!' He looked straight at us, challenging us to see just how terrified we were. Then he tossed the key into the dark, and grinned.

I glanced at Matt and saw him already studying the map. He was quiet the entire time, and I then realized that there was nothing to be done there at the gate—we were stuck there for the night, at least. But I was still worried about Karen. Will wasn't there, so he must have taken her out of the cave already, and I wanted to know what was happening to her.

'Where's Karen? What did you do to her?' I demanded.

'That's none of your business, little man. Let's just say she's safe with Will—for now.' Then he stared straight into my eyes and said, 'Ok, boys, good night! Don't let, well, anything bite!'

Jason thought his joke was very funny, his whole body shaking and the Main Hall echoing with his laughter.

22

I juddered the locked gate one more time, more to let out some of the frustration than really expecting it to open. How could this be happening? We were locked inside a cave with a million bats and no food. Matt only had a small bottle of water stuck in his side pocket, and that was it. But the worst thing was that my parents had no idea we were down here. I started screaming for help, but decided it was no use— nobody would hear us down there in the middle of the night. The security guy had probably been asleep for some time now, back at his post in the mansion. We only had two options—accept Jason's challenge and try finding our way out through a room full of bats, or wait for the morning and hope someone heard us. But I turned to Matt and said, 'I'm not going anywhere near those bats! I'm not going in the Nursery, or whatever it's called. I just won't go in there!'

'Maybe we don't have to—look!' Matt turned his phone flashlight off and took the flashlight out of my hands. 'We're here, right?' He pointed to our location on the more and more unreadable, dirty map.

'Yes?' I said, impatiently.

'And this is the Nursery, right?'

'Right.'

'So, we could go back up this tunnel and turn left here into that small corridor, through the Nursery, and into this tunnel on the far side of it.' Matt was explaining the route as he followed it with his finger.

'I'm not going through there. No way,' I said again.

'In which case we can only hope those two jerks didn't lock the gate on that tunnel too,' he added.

'True,' I nodded.

'But look at this—see where this tunnel is going?' Matt used his finger as a pointer again, and followed the tunnel from where we stood, away from the Nursery, and further up.

His finger went past the spot where we'd found the diamond and continued to follow the tunnel until it started turning back toward the Main Hall, just around the Nursery. The map was completely unreadable in that spot, so we couldn't really tell if the tunnel went all the way back to the Main Hall, or maybe it joined the second corridor leading away from the Nursery. But it was worth a shot. I only had one big concern. The map showed the tunnel we were in now narrowing down once it went past the tiny diamond sketch. I hoped it was only because the map was hand drawn—a human mistake.

'I'm ok with that. I would rather try that, and come right back here if we can't get through, than go in that bat-infested room,' I said.

'Yeah. Me too. Let's go and check it out,' Matt said, and we turned and went back up the tunnel, and into the thick, foul air.

Once we got past the corridor to the Nursery, I stopped and took out the diamond from my pocket. Even being locked up below the surface couldn't take away the beauty of the thing, glistening in my dirty, sweaty hand. Matt gave me a glance, and we both smiled, for the first time since we had actually found the island's greatest treasure. Matt took it from my hand, and looked closely at it, while I held the light for him. Whatever happens, I thought, we wouldn't give this thing away. Who knows how valuable it actually is—maybe my parents would forgive me when they see what we brought back?

We shuffled along, my eyes now totally used to the darkness, and being able to see pretty much everything with just the one flashlight we had.

'What do you think happened to Karen?' Matt asked, clearly worried about her.

'I don't know,' I said, 'but I'm pretty sure she'll be ok. Those two guys are jerks, but they're not idiots. They won't hurt her or anything. And besides—she's tough, probably tougher than we are, so . . . she'll be ok,' I hoped.

The tunnel curved right for a short while, but then turned back left, and looped around the Nursery. *So far, so good*, I thought, but then I had a chilling realization. The walls had started to close in on us, and the ceiling came down to the point where I had to crouch down to continue forward. The tunnel was narrowing down, and we had no way of knowing if we'd be able to continue.

23

'I don't like this,' I said, shuffling along, hunkered down, trying not to hit my head on the rocky ceiling. 'Hope it gets wider soon, or we'll just have to go back.'

The thought of going back made me disappointed and downhearted. Back to where, exactly? There was nowhere back to go, except all the way to the locked gate. There we could only sit and wait for somebody to come down and rescue us. Not exactly what I wanted to happen, but it wasn't like we had a choice. Matt said nothing, he just trudged along with me—actually behind me—as there was no more room to walk side by side.

But things weren't getting any better, like I'd hoped. The tunnel suddenly stopped altogether, and turned to not much more than a two-foot crack in a solid rock wall.

I stooped down and shone the light through

the hole. The light beam went straight through a short, narrow crack, and rested on some kind of a rock wall on the other side. It looked like we could go through it, but just the thought of it made my stomach churn and my legs weak and wobbly.

'Let me see,' Matt said behind me, and then took the flashlight to take a look for himself. 'I think we can squeeze through. Looks like there's more space on the other side,' he said, and then turned to me, 'You in?'

I didn't want to be 'in'. I wanted to be back at the cabin, in my top bunk bed, sound asleep. But instead, I was in a dark cave, seriously thinking about sliding my body through a crack in the rock, all dirty and tired, not knowing when I'd be getting out, if ever. We still weren't panicking, but I thought that it might be a good time to start.

I exhaled. Sighed, really. *C'mon, Ethan, you can do this!* I said to myself, not sure if I believed it or not. But Matt knew me well. He understood right away that I was terrified of possibly getting stuck in there, not being able to move. He knew I didn't like tight spaces. So he waited for a long moment before finally saying, 'It's ok, don't worry about it. We'll just go back and wait.

Someone will come and get us soon.'

Not saying a word more, he'd already turned to go back. He was that kind of a friend. So I couldn't just let him down and not even try to go forward.

I took a deep breath, straightened my shoulders, and said, 'You know what? Let's do this. I'm ready!' And I spun around to go through first, before I lost my nerve.

'Ok,' Matt said, and turned back to face the crack.

I gave the flashlight to Matt, so I'd have both hands free, and slowly crawled into the crack. The rock was moist, which I guess helped me to slide along. Both of my arms were stretched forward, and I pushed myself through the crack with my feet. I kept my head down, only my eyes were trying to look up to see where I was going. I was sweating again, and my breathing was shallow, as if I could feel the weight of the earth pressing down on my body.

About half-way through, my right shoulder got stuck and wouldn't move. Air came rushing out of my lungs in one big sigh, and I felt my mind starting to spiral into blackness.

'You ok?' Matt called from behind me.

The sound of his voice helped me get it

together, so I finally opened my eyes and said, 'I'm stuck.'

'Hold on, let me try pushing you.'

'Ok, but wait a second, let me try shifting my shoulders first,' I said, and tried to slide my body to the left, to release my stuck right shoulder. Thankfully, there was a bit more space there, and I could feel my right shoulder freeing up.

'Ok, push now!'

Matt pushed the soles of my feet, and finally I was through the tight bottleneck. He crawled in right behind me, and as soon as I wriggled myself out of the crack, I took the flashlight from him, and pulled his hands to help him to the other side.

As we both stood up at the other end, we immediately sensed a spine-chilling, dreadful change in the air. Even without illuminating the ceiling and the walls around us, I could sense the movement, as if the place itself was alive. The nauseating stench of bats was worse, much worse, and it didn't just stop at my nose—I could actually taste the pungent air in my mouth. The fluttering of tiny, leathery wings grew much louder, and felt much closer to us.

There was no way of mistaking it for anything else. I closed my eyes and my shoulders slumped in defeat as I realized the horrible truth—we had ended up in the Nursery.

24

I felt a strange calmness washing over me as I opened my eyes to have a better look around. I guess by that point I was simply done being afraid, and I just didn't care what else the cursed cave might throw at us.

'Should we go back?' Matt asked, but I knew by the sound of his voice, that he felt the same way as I did, and wanted to keep moving.

'No, I'm good. You ok?'

'Yeah,' he said, and pulled the map out of his shorts pocket. 'Ok, so I guess this is where we're at now. And this is where we need to get to,' he pointed at the far side of the room, at the second tunnel leading away from it, and towards the Main Hall. 'We could have already been there by now, but no point crying over it now.'

I agreed with him. We'd ended up in the exact place we hoped we wouldn't have to be in, but there was nothing to be done about it. So we took a few steps away from the small lobby we were standing in, and marched straight into the room.

The room was full of bats. Bats hanging from the ceiling, perched on the rocky bumps on the walls, some of them even crawling along on the room floor. As I scanned the room with my flashlight, we could see tiny pinkish bat pups, clustered together in small groups, sometimes all alone, sometimes protected by their mother's thin, almost see-through wings. I couldn't even imagine how these bat moms found their pups after returning to the cave. I guessed maybe the pups didn't smell as bad as the rest of the population in there.

But the worst part of the whole scene was set on the rock floor, right in the middle of the room. The floor seemed to be alive and pulsating and quivering. Squirming, huge worms were wriggling though the dark, soil-like mass that must have been bat poop. And there was tons of it, several feet tall in the middle of the floor, like some organic mountain. And on the slopes of that mountain, there was a dead bat here and there, and they were all being swarmed by huge, fast-moving beetles.

I was disgusted by the spectacle, but still

determined to get through this. So I started looking for a way out. Off to the left, I noticed a narrow, natural pathway between the wall and the mountain of bat poop in the middle. Up close to the ceiling the wall curved inward, creating some sort of an umbrella shelter, leaving a clean stretch of rocky floor.

I motioned to Matt to follow me, and I started down the narrow path, careful not to step onto anything moving on the floor. As we shuffled along, we disturbed a couple of bats perched on the bulges on the wall to our left. They fluttered their wings and flew away angrily, annoyed by being woken up by the intruders. I actually started to respect the little devils, and hoped that the respect was mutual. I didn't want to end up being a part of the feeding frenzy on the floor of that room.

We kept moving. Sliding along the wall, drenched in our own sweat. *What did Karen say— the bats stay here because it's the warmest room*? It sounded about right. I didn't talk—I had nothing to say. Matt didn't talk because, well, because he was Matt. I tried to hold my breath as much as I could, and then inhale through a paper tissue I'd pulled out of my pocket. It helped to reduce the foul stench a little. Matt trudged behind me, his phone flashlight illuminating my feet as he tried to follow the path. Needless to say, we both kept our light beams straight ahead, trying hard not to see the horrors on the floor a few feet away to the right.

Matt almost slammed into my back when I stopped. I looked up from the floor at the smooth rock wall right in front of me, the light beam from the flashlight following my gaze.

'What is it?', Matt whispered from behind. 'Why did you stop?'

'There's a wall. I think the path ends here,' I said, my voice trembling, and I felt like I was finally going to lose my nerve.

But then, as I stepped closer to the wall, smooth enough not to have any bats perched on it, I saw that it turned sharply left again. I peeped around the corner, and sighed in relief.

'All good. It's still here. The path goes on.'

'Let's get a move on, I'm getting dizzy, and I'm about to throw up,' Matt said, and I knew exactly how he felt.

Soon we walked past the corridor to the tunnel from which we came in the first place. At that point the path widened, and there were fewer bats around or above us. The other exit corridor was now in sight, and we hurried along the wall to it.

'Good thing we took the long way round to get here,' Matt chuckled, obviously not letting me forget it was me who insisted on trying to find another way out.

'Just imagine, we wouldn't have seen all those wonders of nature on the floor back there!' he continued. 'And now we know we don't have to go on a diet—we're thin enough to squeeze through anywhere!'

'Ok, you can shut up now,' I said, but grinning at him. He shrugged, and grinned, and then we shuffled along, faster now, toward the far side of the Nursery. The air was already getting cooler, and I could feel the welcoming breeze of much fresher, sweeter air on my face as we stepped off the path and entered the corridor. The short corridor led to a larger tunnel, and we knew from the map that if we took a left turn here, we'd be seeing the Main Hall soon. And we did, after a minute or two of skipping down the tunnel. It wasn't a happy moment, though—the Main Hall was waiting for us on the other side of a closed barred gate, right behind Jason who was about to put a big padlock on it.

25

Sometimes, when you're pushed to the limit, the world seems to slow down around you, and everything becomes incredibly clear. I knew immediately that I couldn't let him lock the door, so I flung myself toward the gate with everything I had in me. I ran into the gate full speed, leading with my shoulder, and I could see the surprise in Jason's eyes the split second before the impact as he started backing away awkwardly.

The blow was colossal, and it hurt like hell, but I got the job done, and the gate hit Jason right in the chest and sent him flying onto his back a few feet away. When my shoulder hit the gate, I realized why Jason couldn't close it all the way and lock it. The grinding sound coming from the rusty hinges made it clear that the gate was half-stuck.

While Jason was on his back, shocked and trying to wriggle himself back onto his feet, like some kind of a giant turtle, I saw Will already rushing down from the other side of the Main Hall, from the main entrance. They both looked enraged, and I didn't want to be there to ask them why.

'Start closing the gate, and get back in the tunnel!' I yelled, hoping that Matt would understand what I was trying to do. I twisted and leapt toward the gate, took off the still unlocked padlock, and slid past the half-closed gate.

'Let's go, quick, follow me!' I breathed, while helping Matt to shut the gate. 'That'll give us a few seconds!'

'That was awesome! You ok?' Matt said, as we ran back up the tunnel.

'Yeah. My shoulder is killing me, but I'll be ok.'

'What's your plan?'

'Not sure, but I didn't want them to lock us in. Maybe now we can find a place to hide, or at least to throw away the padlock.'

We could already hear the squeaking of the rusty hinges behind us, and the angry voices of Jason and Will. They wouldn't let us off the hook that easily, that was for sure.

'Maybe I have an idea. Come on!' I said, and started running down the corridor and back into the Nursery. Jason and Will followed, getting closer.

We ran past the bats, and straight out to the other tunnel. Then we turned left and back up, toward the narrow crack.

'Yes! That might work!' Matt puffed at my side. Now he saw what I was thinking, and he was on board.

'I hope so. Karen said they know a lot about the caves, but maybe they'll be too mad to stop and think,' I said, running as fast as I could.

They followed, and when we reached the narrow crack, they were not far behind. Matt went first this time, and I stayed back, looking over my shoulder, which still hurt from the blow.

'Come on, hurry up!' I urged him, and then squeezed myself into the crack. I started crawling and saw Matt already stepping out on the Nursery floor. Then, my leg wouldn't move anymore.

'No you won't!' Jason cried behind me, as he grabbed my ankle.

'Matt! Pull me!' I said, as I kicked my leg as much as I could in the narrow space. I stretched my arms forward, and grabbed onto Matt's hands. He pulled as hard as he could, and I felt Jason's hold on my foot slipping.

I was free, and back inside the Nursery.

I peered through the gap, and blew Jason a kiss, trying to enrage him even further. It worked like a charm, and he charged down the narrow passageway like a raging bull, Will right behind him.

'They took the bait! They're coming through the crack after us!' I said to Matt. He knew exactly what that meant. 'That'll slow them down—it's a shame they're so big and wide,' I winked.

'Awesome! Good plan, well executed!' Matt was grinning as we started running back to the gate at the Main Hall.

Which was a huge mistake.

Firstly, because the rock floor was damp and slippery, so I stumbled and fell, and I slid across the floor, my face stopping literally an inch from the mountain of bat poop.

Secondly, unlike the first time we went through the Nursery, we weren't being calm and quiet. Or moving slowly. Which the bats didn't appreciate. Suddenly, the whole room fluttered loudly and the air quivered with the excited flapping of a thousand leathery wings.

I screamed, covered my head with my hands, ducked, and ran as fast as my legs would take me. Matt was right behind me, and he was screaming too. Huge bats were flying frantically right over our heads, and I could feel the wind made by their wings. I did not dare to look up. Only out of the corner of my eye I could see bats flying toward my head, and then turning away incredibly quickly like tiny, dark fighter jets, just before they smashed into me. I was sure Matt was going to tell me all about how the little furry winged beasts pulled that off. Up ahead, the trail we used before was clearly visible, and I could already see the way out.

We just kept moving. I don't know whether it was the rush and the excitement of fleeing, but I think both Matt and I broke some kind of world record getting ourselves back down the corridor to the Main Hall. Luckily for us, the bats decided to remain in the Nursery. On the other hand, the sound of Jason and Will screaming in terror coming from the bat-infested room told me they were not so lucky.

26

Over the next few moments, I experienced the biggest emotional turmoil of my life. We ran the last few paces toward the gate, and pushed it open, just enough to squeeze ourselves out.

'You still have the padlock, right?' Matt said, breathing heavily from all the running.

'Yes, and I think we should use it, don't you think?'

Not wasting any time at all, we spun around and pushed the gate shut. The hinges must have loosened up from when I ran into it. I took the padlock from my pocket and put it on the gate. It locked with a satisfying metallic click, and I slowly stepped a few paces back as the realization of what we'd just done sunk in.

We'd locked Jason and Will inside the caves, with the bats, and the diamond was still in my pocket.

'You think they'll be all right?' I said, suddenly

feeling sorry for the two poor souls.

'Who knows? I don't really care—you don't think they'd be having the same feelings for us, do you?! But I'll tell you one thing. I'm so happy to be out of those tunnels! I have no idea how you managed to keep your cool and get us out of there, but thanks anyway!' Matt said.

I stood there, staring at him, my mouth wide open in shock. *Did he really just say all that*?! And not just the 'thanks' part, but in so many words? There might be a human in him after all, I thought. Then we got as sappy as two boys like us could ever get—we even patted each other's back after a loud, cracking high-five. Lame, right? I should never mention this ever again!

As we heard Jason and Will's voices coming from the dark of the tunnel, we turned toward the Main Hall to get our bearings. Off to the right, at the top of a gentle slope, we could see a little bit of glowing light coming from the outside.

'The main entrance!' I cried, and we started running up toward it. The slope was still a bit slippery, but it was also nice, gentle and wide, no iron ladders or anything like that. No wonder it was used for tourists and old, rich people.

The pale moonlight felt as bright as the sunniest

of days as we leapt out from underground, and into the delicious, cool, fresh air. Both Matt and I knew that we could still be in danger, so we carefully scanned the outside of the main entrance, just to make sure there were no friends of Jason and Will's lurking in the shadows. Once satisfied that we were alone and safe, I pulled the diamond out of my pocket again. It was even prettier and more mystical in the silvery moonlight, and I couldn't help but wonder what we should do with it.

'We should go. Maybe we can find out what happened to Karen,' Matt pointed out.

I snapped out of thinking about the diamond, and nodded in agreement. There was no time for a victory dance, or moonlight-dreaming about the diamond. And I really wanted to get away from the island, and never set foot on it ever again.

'Yeah. And I think we should send someone back first thing in the morning to let those two out! Maybe call the security guy or something,' I said, still feeling bad for them.

'Ok. You're right. I was just mad at them. Still am. But nobody deserves to be locked up in there for too long,' Matt said, and we got moving again.

We hurried down the gravel pathway around the island, this time not caring at all if we were heard or seen by the security guy. At that point, he could have only been of help to us, if we ran into him. But we didn't, so we jogged all the way to the dock.

'The canoe is still here!' Matt cried, almost surprised to find our boat exactly where we'd left it.

'I don't think Jason and Will wanted to take it or hide it. If they did, we could prove that someone was here messing with us, and then they wouldn't be able to just deny everything,' I said, after giving it some thought.

'But where's their boat? How did they get here?'

'I don't know. Maybe Karen got away and took it!' I said.

'Look—are those canoe tracks in the sand over there?' Matt said, pointing toward some fresh tracks in the sand.

'Looks like it. They must've sent her back home. Let's go, maybe we can still catch up with her, to see if she's alright!'

Either way, we weren't going to lose any more time on the island, so we climbed into the canoe and started paddling hard.

As we left the illuminated island behind us and entered the inky darkness of the middle of the lake, I noticed the orange glow of a small campfire on the beach in front of us.

'Here we go—I'll bet you anything it's the cousins' friends. Why can't they just leave us alone?' I muttered in the dark. 'Maybe Karen is there. She better not be hurt—'

'I don't think they'd hurt her. If she's there at all,' Matt said, 'but we might need to be ready to fight our way back to the cabin to get your mom and dad.'

He was right. We might need to try to get my parents, but I hated that idea. I didn't want them to know anything about this whole night.

We paddled on, and soon we were almost at the beach. As we got closer and closer, still shrouded by the darkness, we stared ahead in disbelief. The scene on the beach was like from the movies—a bunch of kids sitting around the campfire, laughing, talking loudly, high-fiving each other. I recognized most of them as Jason and Will's friends from yesterday. *Was it really only yesterday when we first saw them on the beach?*

'Great. They're all here. Let's just get this over with, I'm not running away again,' Matt muttered.

But I barely heard what he said. My eyes were locked onto Karen who was sitting right there, in the middle of the group. Good thing was, she didn't seem to be hurt or in any kind of danger at all. The bad thing was, she looked cheerful, grinning with the others, enjoying the whole thing, like she was a big part of it.

27

The canoe scraped the sand on the bottom of the lake quietly, as we finally reached the beach. The kids around the campfire spun around to see us hopping out on dry land. Loud cheering disturbed the still night, followed by an uncontrolled roar of laughter. We were the unwilling stars of the show, and I didn't like it one bit.

'Diamond hunters! Cavemen!' Were some of the chants I managed to hear, all followed by the mocking applause of the others.

We stood there, bewildered, not knowing what to do next, or where to go. My eyes locked with Karen's, looking for some explanation, but those green eyes seemed completely different. There was malice in them, and contempt, and some sort of pride. I couldn't understand where that came from, but it made me realise that I needed to protect the diamond.

'We lost the diamond back at the island, just

so you know. It fell out of my pocket and you'll never find it again!' I cried, but the reaction I got was completely unexpected. Some kids started laughing so hard they were rolling on the ground, holding their bellies, totally out of control. Karen stood up.

A smug, wide grin on her face she said, 'I don't think you did. I think it's still in one of your pockets. But it doesn't really matter. You see, that thing is a fake!'

What?! *A fake*?!

'But,—why?' I stuttered.

More guffaws from the campfire.

'Why? Because it was fun!' Karen exclaimed, a huge grin on her face. 'We try to pull this off every summer, but you two . . . Congratulations! You two went further than anyone else. You actually went all the way!'

'What do you mean 'every summer'?' I demanded. I could feel my confusion and disappointment with Karen being slowly replaced with honest, old-fashioned anger.

She smirked at me, pride in her changed, totally cold and unfamiliar voice, and said, 'That's why it was planned to perfection, if you don't mind my saying. From planting the key, the map, the page out of the diary—everything. All the way down to timing and signals! If we couldn't find the real diamond, maybe we could at least get some fun out of that story!' The kids around the campfire nodded, grins not leaving their faces.

Suddenly I didn't feel bad for locking her cousins in with the bats anymore.

'I see you managed to escape the caves. Bravo!' she snickered. 'Where are Jason and Will?' she said as she peered into the darkness over the lake, expecting to see her cousins right behind us.

'I wouldn't expect to see them any time soon. They might be exploring the caves in depth, if you know what I mean.' I said, and showed her the padlock key from my pocket. I made sure she got a good look at it before I hurled it as far into the lake as I could.

She stared at me for a long moment, and then simply said, 'Doesn't matter. They'll be alright. But did you really think that a couple of city boys like you would find such a treasure, when all those people before you failed?' She sneered, laughing the idea away.

I glanced at Matt, still not believing what was happening. He just stood there, calm, quiet, his hands in his pockets. I thought this was his 'stand-by' mode. I turned my gaze back at Karen and swallowed hard. My mouth was so dry, I was sure I could drink the whole lake and still be thirsty.

'So you're telling us that we risked our lives in that cave for nothing? This is worthless?!' I almost screamed, incredulous, as I held out the thing I had believed was a diamond until then.

Karen stepped toward me.

'Let me answer it this way,' she said.

She grabbed the 'diamond' out of my hand, placed it on a boulder next to the campfire, picked up a large stone and swung it high over her head.

28

As the fake diamond shattered into a hundred small pieces of glass, I felt a pang of sadness, even though now I knew for sure that it wasn't real. But I still wanted to keep it—if nothing else, as a reminder to be careful who to trust. I felt sad and defeated when I raised my eyes to look at Matt.

'I'm sorry,' I said. 'I brought you all the way to this damn lake. It's all my fault.'

'No, it isn't. And don't worry about it—we're cool,' Matt said, cool as a cucumber.

I turned back to face all of them. I stared straight into Karen's eyes and said in a clear voice, 'You're all jerks, you know that? Have fun now, we're leaving.'

As we shuffled to pull the canoe further up the beach, a familiar raspy voice rang out over the giggles and snickers of the group around the fire.

'That's enough!' Ms. Davenport, Karen's grandmother said.

To my utter horror, Mom and Dad were standing right behind her, disbelief and anger on their faces.

'I will not have this! I will not wake up in the middle of the night to find your beds empty. I will be calling your parents first thing in the morning!' Ms. Davenport pointed her wrinkled, bony finger at Karen. 'I believe you have some explaining to do, young lady. I'm sure this was all your idea.'

Mom and Dad motioned to us to join them. From up close, I couldn't really tell if they were more mad, or disappointed in me. I was sure Matt would be ok—they'll say it was all my fault.

It soon became clear that Mom was furious.

'You boys are so grounded! You won't leave your room until the end of this weekend, and then some! What the heck happened here? Who are all these kids?'

Before we could answer any of my mom's questions, Ms. Davenport turned around to share what she'd heard from Karen. I was sure that Karen would not shy away from her 'accomplishment', and that she wouldn't leave out any of the 'brilliant' details.

'The boys were chasing a legend,' she said to Mom and Dad, her eyes mild and understanding. 'Karen, my granddaughter, and her cousins, tricked the boys into believing they'd found a treasure map. Ethan and Matt just wanted to have an adventure—you can't really blame them for that.'

I wanted to leap and hug the old lady and thank her for being on our side. There was no chance that we could avoid my mom's fury, but at least she could understand why we did it. Mom just gave me a sideways glance.

'But you boys should have read a bit more about the Davenport diamond. It would have saved you a lot of trouble. That is to say, while nobody knows where the diamond ended up, we do know what it looked like. And it didn't look like that shiny, polished thing I saw in pieces over there by the fire,' she said, and pointed to the shattered remains of the fake.

'No,' she continued, 'the Dead-end Island diamond was uncut.'

'Uncut? As in, not shaped or polished smooth and shiny?' Matt wanted to know the details. Of course he did, he had probably read something about it in his precious book. I couldn't believe he was talking about rocks and geology at a time like that. I thought he should show a bit more emotion. Some anger, or disappointment at the very least. But he looked almost excited by that conversation, as excited as he could ever get.

'Exactly!' Ms. Davenport agreed. 'The real diamond was uncut, but very clear, almost bright white with just a hint of a yellow hue. It was also shaped like a heart. All that made it so very rare and valuable.'

'What do you mean, 'shaped like a heart'?' I wondered.

She gave me a long gentle stare before she answered, 'My dear boy, why do you think they called it the Heart of the Island?'

29

The campfire had almost burned out, but the kids were still standing around it in a semicircle, now listening to Ms. Davenport's story. She turned and sent them all home, making sure that they knew she'd be talking to their families in the morning. When she learned from me and Matt what had happened to her other grandchildren, Jason and Will, and that they were locked in the caves on the island, she nodded in agreement—almost patted our backs. I guess she didn't really like them either.

'Karen, you're coming home with me right now! Get in the car!' She said to her, and turned back to face my parents.

'I am really sorry for what happened here, and I do apologize for my family. Good night to you all, I hope you'll be able to put this behind you and forgive us.' She then nodded, spun around, and started walking toward the road.

As they were leaving the beach, Karen Davenport wore a proud grin on her face, plainly pleased and very satisfied with what they'd done. Just before she vanished into the trees, she tuned to us one last time, and waved a mocking good-bye.

***

Matt and I followed Mom and Dad to the cabin in sullen silence. We both knew we'd messed up, and that we were going to be grounded forever—well, at least I knew I would be. But being fooled and deceived by the Davenports hurt much more than that. I felt like a complete dummy.

When we got back to the cabin, Dad closed the door and spoke for the first time since we'd seen Mom and him on the beach.

'Boys, that was a reckless, silly and dangerous thing to do. But—I get it. I do understand why you went along with it. And I'm really sorry you two got hoaxed like that.'

'Thanks, Dad,' I muttered, glad to see that he wasn't super mad at me after all.

'Now I've got to go and get ready for fishing, but your mom and I will discuss your punishment when I get back later in the morning. You two—

take a quick shower, and go to bed. Now.'

I didn't need to be told twice. I was tired and grimy and filthy. It took Matt and me less than five minutes to shower and get into our beds. Once in bed, my mind started racing, and I wasn't sure if I'd be able to fall asleep. My whole body was still tense and my teeth were clenched.

I heard Matt still squirming on his bottom bunk.

'How could we be so stupid?' I muttered through my teeth.

'You know what? Maybe we weren't so stupid, after all,' Matt replied, sounding annoyingly cheerful.

'Yeah, yeah . . . I'm sure we learned a valuable lesson or something,' I said, irritated by him. 'I'm also sure we will be laughed at for years to come. Maybe they will be telling stories about us, sitting around campfires. They'll call it 'The Legend of Two Knuckleheads'!'

'I'm not so sure about that, either,' Matt said. 'You remember that pile of stuff that spilled out of the cabinets of the old desk at the helipad? When we were hiding from the security guy?'

'Yes. What about it?' I said, impatiently. I remembered putting a leather-bound notebook in my pocket to look for new information. I also remembered tossing it right back into the pile of furniture as we raced toward our canoe after we locked the Davenports in the cave. I was pretty sure Matt did the same.

'Well, I threw away the notebooks—I figured there was nothing in them worth reading, but I kept something I picked up, something that looked interesting—'

'So? What was it? What did you find?'

'So, I didn't give it too much thought, until I heard what Ms. Davenport said at the beach. About the diamond. And how it looked. Because—this is what I carried in my pocket the whole time we were down there in the caves . . .'

I leaned out of the top bunk, and saw Matt's outstretched arm. His hand was open, and on his palm there was a leather pouch, one that I remembered seeing before that night, at the helipad, behind the broken desk.

Resting on the leather pouch was something that looked like an egg-sized rock. It was shaped like a heart, and I didn't need the light to know that it was white in color, with just a hint of a yellow hue.

30

'Mom! Wake up! Come, take a look at this!' I didn't even knock on the door as I hurled myself in my parents' bedroom. Mom jumped up in bed, startled, her face twisted in fear.

'What happened?! Are you ok?' she cried.

'Yes, we're fine. We're GREAT! Look!' I held out the diamond for her to see. Matt was standing behind me in the doorframe, too polite to enter the room uninvited.

'What is that? Is that—, could that be—' Mom muttered. 'Let me see that!' she took the diamond out of my hand, gently, carefully, as if not to break it or drop it on the floor. 'How did you get this? Where did you find it?'

Matt and I told her the whole story again, this time including all the important bits, and as we told it, I couldn't believe just how lucky we got in the end. Who would have thought that such a great treasure was hiding in plain sight this whole time.

'Guys, this is awesome!' Dad said when he got back. 'I always wanted to find a treasure when I was a kid!' he exclaimed, beaming like a little boy. 'But I really don't think we should keep it, or sell it. It wouldn't be right—it belongs in a museum.'

'I agree,' Mom said, 'It belonged to the Davenport family, and, even if they don't deserve to look after it, we shouldn't have it either.'

I glanced at Matt, and we silently agreed with them. I mean, what else were we supposed to do? My parents made a lot of sense, and neither Matt nor I had any better ideas.

The rest of the morning went by like a blur. We visited the police station to declare our find, and Dad talked to his lawyer friend on the phone to arrange a donation with the museum. Then, Mom called Mrs. Davenport to tell her what happened. Mom wanted her to hear it from us, not from the news or gossip. She invited us all to her house, so we could talk about everything over cake and lemonade.

'I have to say—I'm relieved. I'm glad that someone other than my own family found the cursed thing, and I think you're doing the right thing donating it to the museum,' Luisa

Davenport said in her raspy voice, looking very relaxed, as if some weight had been lifted from her shoulders. 'I had my doubts, but what happened last night convinced me that nobody in my family deserves such wealth and fortune!'

Karen, on the other hand, was not so graceful about the news. Ms Davenport made her go back to the island in the morning, carrying nothing more than a bolt cutter to cut through the padlocks and let Jason and Will out. They came back right at the time when we were finishing cake out on the porch. It was a sad spectacle—I could see just how hungry and thirsty and miserable the two jerks were, and their looks weren't great, either. I couldn't help but feel sorry for them, again.

'What are you two doing here?' Karen said, slowly, her eyes darting between her grandmother and my parents.

Jason and Will just stood there, quietly. All three of them immediately knew something was going on; something they wouldn't like, even before Ms. Davenport stood up and told them the whole story.

'Grandma! You can't let them have it! Give it to me! It's ours! It's—*mine*!'

The last word she cried still echoed in my mind,

as she burst into tears, and her legs gave way. She fell on her knees and sobbed uncontrollably. Jason and Will stared at Karen on the ground, saying nothing, their shoulders slumped, their heads hanging limply, chins on their chests. I realized just how obsessed Karen and her cousins were with the Heart of the Island, and I was sure that deciding to give the diamond to a museum was the right thing to do.

Before we left the house, my eyes locked with Jason's for a brief moment, and I thought I saw him nod a little, as if saying 'good bye'. It felt like he accepted our decision, and I hoped that this would be the end of their exhausting, unhealthy obsession.

31

The morning of the photoshoot came quickly. Matt and I were in my living room, playing a video game, waiting for my mom to get ready and take us to the museum. The curator of the museum insisted we had to be there for the Heart of the Island handover ceremony, and he wanted us to take pictures with the diamond in front of the museum. The story about two boys finding such a treasure spread like wildfire throughout the country, and the media was impressed by our decision to donate it. There was a nice catch though, something the curator kept as a secret from everybody. He insisted that Matt and I should be rewarded with a large finder's fee, and that the museum would set up a trust fund in our names. Fine by me, I thought, although the fund would be managed by our parents. No new bicycle coming any time soon, sadly.

'Mom! You ready? We're gonna be late!' I

cried out.

She came down the stairs, all dressed up and ready to go. She glanced at the mirror in the hallway one last time, to make sure everything was in place, then we climbed into the car, Matt and I in the back.

The photoshoot was over quickly – the whole thing took about a minute. There was also a news reporter and a cameraman from the local TV station, wanting to talk to us.

'What can you tell us about your plans now?' the TV guy said.

'Well, now we're on the lookout for our next adventure! We're opening our hotline for all the kids out there who need help with anything!' I joked. Matt didn't say anything, of course.

After that we watched the diamond being put in a thick glass box, and then we were ushered out so the museum staff could do whatever it was they needed to do.

***

The next day, Matt came to my house early. He was really excited about something and
he wanted to talk.

'Did you see the news today? On TV? We're all

over the place! And our picture at the museum is everywhere in the newspapers!' he said.

'Yeah, I saw it. So what?' I yawned, still wearing my pj's.

'Did you check your phone? I got some texts from kids I don't know. They all want us to come and help them out with things, problems they can't figure out on their own—to solve some mysteries, or find treasure, or just, you know—help them figure stuff out!' Matt rambled, totally out of character.

I checked my phone real quick, and saw that he was right. I had at least a dozen messages on my phone. Some of them were just my friends saying that they'd seen us on TV, but some of them were actual requests, just like Matt said. It seemed like we'd become popular.

'But, how are we going to help them? I mean, these kids live all over the country. We can't just go traveling around like that! What about school?' I wondered.

'School is out now, right? And there are always weekends,' Matt said.

'That could work,' I said. 'And I think my dad would be ok with it. He might even give me some of the trust money to spend on traveling. We proved we can do it, right?'

'So, you're in? We're doing this?' Matt pushed, suddenly looking like a puppy waiting for its owner to give him a treat.

I started warming up to the idea. It would be great to go around on adventures like that. We just needed a name to make our little agency official. Something that would make us look serious. Something a comic book might be named after.

'Yes. Let's do this. And I've got a name for this little project of ours,' I agreed. 'Let's call it **'PROJECT ADVENTURE'**.'

ABOUT THE AUTHOR

David is an author of adventure books for middle grade children and anyone who still feels like a kid. He always wanted to write, but couldn't really find the time or the motivation until he and his family started moving around Europe, looking for the right place to settle. In his quest to entertain the young audience, David aims to take his readers on an action-packed, fun-filled and mysterious ride in the world he created for his thrill-seeking characters. When not writing or reading, he spends his time cooking or playing basketball (so long as his knees hold out!), and desperately trying to cope with his own twin boys.

www.davidkonradauthor.com

ACKNOWLEDGEMENTS

I would like to thank everyone who helped to write or publish this book. It was challenging work, and I am thrilled how it all turned out. First of all, big thanks to my family on selfless support and understanding. To my editors, Anna and Grace, on their effort and advice, and making it seem like I knew what I was doing, and to my art director Sarah on her passion to turn my manuscript into a proper book. Thank you Dion for the beautiful cover illustration and your creativity. Last, but not least, a big thanks to Heather for the valuable tips on how to promote this book and bring it closer to the readers.

READY FOR MORE STORIES?

Now that you've finished **HEART OF THE ISLAND**, why not join my mailing list to continue the adventure and be alerted when new installments are added to the series? This way you'll never miss out on the next exciting adventure!

To become a subscriber, just head on over to:
www.davidkonradauthor.com

OTHER BOOKS BY
DAVID KONRAD

TO BE CONTINUED . . .

Printed in Poland
by Amazon Fulfillment
Poland Sp. z o.o., Wrocław

65525067R00099